DEAD & BURIED

GRAVE TALKER SERIES BOOK SEVEN

ANNIE ANDERSON

DEAD & BURIED
ARCANE SOULS WORLD
Grave Talker Book 7

International Bestselling Author
Annie Anderson

Edited by Angela Sanders
Cover Design by Tattered Quill Designs

www.annieande.com

BOOKS BY ANNIE ANDERSON

THE ARCANE SOULS WORLD

GRAVE TALKER SERIES

Dead to Me

Dead & Gone

Dead Calm

Dead Shift

Dead Ahead

Dead Wrong

Dead & Buried

SOUL READER SERIES

Night Watch

Death Watch

Grave Watch

THE WRONG WITCH SERIES

Spells & Slip-ups

Magic & Mayhem

Errors & Exorcisms

To spite.

You got me through a lot—things I never thought I'd make it through. But I did them. Because of you.

If nothing else works, just remember that spite is just as good a motivator as any.

— ANNIE ANDERSON

I'd always thought it was the dead that would forever be my biggest problem. With the ghosts and lack of privacy and near-constant headaches as souls just would not. Shut. Up. A year ago, those were my biggest problems.

Now, I'd give my left boob to go back to that.

"He's one guy, Sloane." Flicking the cap off my favorite amaretto creamer, I added the blissful concoction to the nectar of life. "Slippery as fuck, sure, but a god he is not. How can the Fates not know where he is? I call bullshit."

Yes, it was eight p.m. on a Wednesday, and no, I did not give a fuck that I was drinking coffee so late. If I didn't drink the happy go-go juice, I would dive head-first into the vodka and never come out.

My sister, however, poured herself a glass of booze and chugged it back like a champ. Then—even though she was an actual goddess—she shivered like she'd never taken a shot before in her life. Rookie.

"Your ex makes our brother look like a saint. Have you looked through these case files?" She lifted a stack of files from the ABI with the redaction spells removed. "Cover-ups, murder, torture, mind control... The more I read, the more I think maybe blood mages should be watched better. *Shit*."

Now that Agent Serreno was gone and Sarina was in charge of the Knoxville ABI, I had been given access to all of Bishop's old cases. The temporary director was the biggest rule-following, stick-up-her-ass, pain in mine since she'd taken the helm, and I was glad she had gone back to Savannah where she could rule that clusterfuck with an iron fist.

But now that I'd dived into these cases, the reading made me sick to my stomach.

Because Bishop was one thing that Nero wasn't: sneaky.

Nero was a dyed-in-the-wool show pony that wanted all eyes on him—wanted anyone and everyone to know exactly how big his dick was. Bishop wanted power under the radar and was quite good at getting it. Considering he had mind-controlled both me and his partner and who knew who else, he was a one-man wrecking ball.

And that was just the shit we knew about.

How many arcaners had ushered the asshole into more and more power? Fifty? A hundred? And who knew if that even scratched the surface?

"You're telling me he disappeared just like that," I griped, stomping my foot, "and you have no idea where he is? You? Of all people? All-seeing, all-knowing Death herself?" I lifted my mug as I shot her a glare over the rim. "Again. Bull. Shit."

How many times had Sloane told me she couldn't tell me the future? Okay, so it was like twice, but it was enough to piss me off.

She poured herself another shot. "You want to talk to the Fates yourself? Be my guest. Personally, I'd love to see you reason with those women."

The thought of waltzing into the Underworld and picking a bone with the women who controlled my future gave me a whole-body shudder. "No, thanks. But I reserve the right to take you up on your offer if things go even more sideways than they already have."

Sloane raised her shot glass and slammed it back. This time her shiver was negligible. "I'm sorry, you know."

Confused, I plopped my cup back on the counter. "For what?"

"For letting you go with him after I knew better—after I knew what he was. I knew it would hurt you, but the outcome would have changed for the worse, and I... I'm glad you got out. I'm sorry I couldn't do more to make that happen faster."

Now I was really in need of that vodka.

Sloane was talking about the fact that there was a very good reason that Bishop La Roux was my ex-boyfriend. Though, calling him that made not one lick of sense. How could one call a man their ex, whose age hit in the five-hundred-plus range, who also manipulated every feeling, thought, and instinct you had?

That wasn't a relationship. It was a hostage situation.

One that ended after he couldn't manipulate me anymore.

"If you want to be all up in your feelings, I'm game. I'll pretend you didn't suggest Jimmy make me the one thing that would free me and offer your assistance at every turn. You're the worst sister ever," I deadpanned. "Totally."

Taking another shot, she flipped me off, and this time, there was nary a shudder.

"Is it customary for Death to be a lush and I forgot, or..."

She rolled her eyes, brushing the white hair that we now shared off her shoulder. "I hate that I can't find this fucker. I told you I'd flip off Fate for you just this once, and when it comes to actually doing it, I bitch out."

It was true: she had told me she'd flip Fate off, but I figured it just meant she'd help me. So what if she couldn't find him?

Okay, so that was a total lie. I was pissed as fuck that we wouldn't find Bishop, but that was on him, not her.

"You know better than that, kiddo."

Sloane shot me a disgusted look over the rim of another shot. "I'm a goddess, you asshole, not a kid."

There was something about that statement that just tickled my funny bone. I had grown up without any siblings—unless you counted Jay, and I sort of did. Having a little sister was new to me. I'd always wanted one, but with my mother faking her death and all, it wasn't like I could squeeze one out of thin air.

"Goddess or not, I was born first, so I will *always* be older. You will forever be a kiddo to me. Deal with it."

Out of the two of us, Sloane being a goddess made the most sense. After her first death almost two years ago, she had been reaping souls one after the other until she was found by the Night Watch. It was only natural for her to do it as a profession, and I'd never been happier that it was not my job.

She stuck out her tongue, probably reading the thoughts only she could hear now that I had Jimmy's handy-dandy necklace. But as much as the necklace protected my mind and body from spells, it didn't cover everything. I still had nightmares about the tunnels under the LeBlanc compound.

About the zombie wolves.

About being swarmed by the dead.

About nearly losing Jay forever.

Not that I'd tell anyone that.

And just as those dark thoughts threatened to pull me under, a presence slammed through all my mental wards, popping into my kitchen, scaring the absolute shit out of me. By the time I recognized who it was, it was already too late. The chaos magic under my skin went off like a damn attack dog, exploding every inch of glass in a hundred-foot radius.

Sloane's bottle of booze? Gone.

All my kitchen cabinets? Toast.

Every condiment in my fridge and every single window in my fucking house? In pieces on my *fucking* floor.

I really needed to get a handle on the *gift* Shiloh had dumped in my lap. But that was after I murdered my already-dead grandfather.

"Hey," Sloane griped, "I was drinking that bottle."

Oh, so slowly I swiveled on a heel, the crunch of broken glass underneath my shoe ominous as I stared Hildy down. This was the *gazillionth* time he'd popped in on me, and I wasn't sure my house—or my sanity—could take much more.

"Hildenbrand, we've talked about this."

My grayed-out, nearly see-through grandfather had his usual top hat and cane in hand, a solid wince on his face. It was true that my jumpiness hadn't gotten any better in the weeks following the attack, and I couldn't even think about what had gone down with Nero. Chaos or not, my mental health wasn't exactly peaches and roses.

"Sorry, lass. Two decades of just showing up has given me some very bad habits."

Hildy had been with me when puberty decided to activate the grave talker gene and bitch-slap me with my ghost-seeing tendencies. Had it not been for him, I would have lost my mind. Then again, if it weren't for him, I wouldn't have a half-exploded house, so there was that.

I was starting to be glad every single one of my neighbors was of the arcane bent. Otherwise, someone would have a lot to say about me blowing shit up every time I got a little too startled.

"Ya really should get ahold on your magic, though. I'd

hate for ya to be out in the field and setting everything ablaze because a ghost gave ya the willies."

"I'm not out in the field, Hildy. I'm in my fucking kitchen. I should be safe in my own kitchen. I should not be on guard here. I should have a moment of security in the one place where I lay my head."

"It's not like you'd die." Sloane pouted on her barstool, swirling her finger in the now-defunct vodka. "You do kinda know a gal in that regard."

I fought the urge to flip them both off. Did it matter that I probably wouldn't die? No. Not at all. Because I knew—just like Sloane did—that dying was easy. Not dying when you absolutely should was a pain in the ass.

Grumbling curses under my breath, I tried to focus the massive power roiling beneath my skin to do something more productive than blowing up my kitchen. Visualizing what it was supposed to look like, I hastily formed the magic to put my house back to rights.

Reverse-entropy spells were the first thing I'd learned in the three months since I'd been bestowed with Shiloh's power. And as someone with no idea how her own abilities worked half the time, witch magic was an enigma wrapped in a cipher, chained in concrete.

The air seemed to shimmer a little until the glass shivered on the floor, moving oh, so slowly until each piece flew back to its home. The slivers formed back into windows and cabinet doors, and the bottle reformed on the counter. Unfortunately, the vodka stayed where it was.

Sweating and breathing heavily, I dug through my freezer, unearthing a new bottle for the pouting goddess. I also may have thrown a dish towel at her head.

"You could have helped, you know."

Sloane pulled the towel off her face, revealing a sly smile. "I know, but how will you practice?"

Asshole.

"I heard that."

"I meant you to."

Hildy—no longer sheepish or apologetic—critiqued my spell. "You missed a window, lass. And your delivery was a little on the slow side. Have you been practicing like I showed ya?"

Grumbling, I snatched the vodka and reformed cup from Sloane and poured myself a shot. "Yes."

"No," Sloane crowed, calling me out on my lie. "She has every intention of *only* using that power under the direst of circumstances. You know how witches make her cranky."

After I drank my shot down, I gave her tattling ass a charged look before stowing the booze right back in the freezer.

"Darby," Hildy chided, drawing out my name like I was a naughty puppy.

"Hildenbrand," I shot back, mocking him. "I've been busy coming up with exactly dick as far as Bishop is concerned. Excuse me for being otherwise occupied."

The eyes of the skull cane in my grandfather's hand glowed green as he drew on its magic. Instantly, he solidified, his chastising glare in full Technicolor. "Bishop La Roux has had five hundred years to master both halves of himself—he knows his magic inside and out. Having power alone won't make it so you can beat him, lass. It's high time you got your head in the game."

I really fucking hated it when Hildy was right.

I hated it more when he was right about me.

"Fine. I'll practice."

Sighing, he released his hold on the corporeal, fading to gray once again. "You can't rely on blind rage and adrenaline, lass. It'll get you killed."

Snorting, I started brewing another pot of coffee, the remnants of the last one all over my counter. I didn't even want to think about the state of my fridge. Taking another deep breath, I worked another spell—this one to clean up my mess. It was really Hildy's mess, but whatever.

Instead of going back to the jars and glasses, the unfortunate liquids decided that the sink was the best home, flowing like ribbons right into the drain, leaving my fridge full of empty bottles and no ketchup or mustard.

Fucking chaos magic. It was as if Puck himself was dicking with me.

Though, when my front door opened, there were no explosions to be had—a real fete since a six-and-a-half-foot elf marched through my door with his sword drawn. At the complete lack of a problem, Jimmy was brought up short. His boyfriend—and my best friend in the world —slammed into his back, narrowly catching him with his talons and fangs.

"Still getting a handle on it, then?" Jimmy remarked, eyebrows raised as his sword winked out of sight.

Rolling my eyes, I replaced the carafe with my coffee mug, praying for it to brew faster. I had no interest in going through a magic intervention because I hadn't been practicing enough.

"I'm fine. It's fine. Everything—except for finding my ex—is fine and fucking dandy. What are you two doing here?"

I rummaged in the fridge, snagging two blood bags and depositing them into the microwave. I was super happy those hadn't exploded, too. When the machine beeped, I tossed them at my best friend—and newly minted vampire—and prayed he'd just let the magic shit go. I could not take a four-way bitch fest.

Jay popped the plastic like a Capri Sun and gave me one of his patented stare-downs as he settled onto a barstool right next to Hildy. Even though he couldn't see my ghostly grandfather, he still shivered when Hildy poked him in the ear, trying to make me smile.

This time, it actually worked.

"Hildy's poking me again, isn't he?" Jay grumbled, switching chairs.

I only gave him my best "butter wouldn't melt in my mouth" smile, re-doctoring my coffee.

"When you volunteered us for this job, I kind of thought it wouldn't be a complete dick punch," Jay began, and it was all I could do not to laugh in his face. "You never said Knoxville was the biggest fucking shitshow known to mankind. I thought Haunted Peak was bad, but... Does the ABI actually do anything about these assholes or—"

My derisive snort was all he needed to hear.

His head thudded to the counter. "When are you coming back?"

Being Warden of Knoxville was an ass pain of the highest order. If it wasn't wolf packs burning down vampire nests, it was ghouls going to war and witches blowing each other up. The ABI had been so corrupt that they'd let ninety percent of the bullshit slide and the other ten was just a way to exert more power.

Cleaning it up had been a full-time job.

My full-time job.

And I'd get back to it. After I found Bishop and punted his severed head into the council's chambers and then took a vacation.

A long one.

Avoiding his question, I asked one of my own. "What's wrong now?"

He rolled his head to the side and shot me a glare. "The Jacobs Coven. Still. You failed to mention how big of a pain in the ass those people were."

Of my list of priorities, the Jacobs Coven had been hovering toward the bottom. Self-policing and barely reactionary, I'd take them nine times out of ten over the Knoxville one I'd disbanded.

And they didn't live in Knoxville.

"The Jacobs Coven is out of your jurisdiction, buddy. Don't borrow trouble."

Jimmy sniffed. "That's what I said."

As usual, Jimmy was right.

The sound of a knock echoed through my house—startling no one except me. A second later, Aemon appeared right next to Sloane, scaring the shit out of Jimmy and Hildy.

Suit impeccable, blond hair windswept, a sexy-as-sin glint in his eyes. But that could mean anything. Naturally, I braced.

"Gird your loins, Flower. I think I have a lead."

As much as I was dying for one of those, somehow that statement coming out of Aemon's mouth was not comforting.

Not. At. All.

2

The problem with Aemon—other than his too-good looks and incessant blithe attitude—was that he was predictably unpredictable. Him having a lead could mean just about anything. And while I desperately needed more than a crumb to go on when it came to Bishop, it was tough to feel warm and fuzzy about whatever it was that he'd come up with.

"Christ on a cracker, demon. Warn someone next time," Hildy griped, adjusting the cravat he'd been wearing since he'd died in the 1840s.

Aemon shot him a sharp eyebrow raise, which tempered his devious smile somewhere around not at all. "What? I knocked first. It's better than what *you* do. I didn't see her explode every window in the house when I came in."

How the fuck did he know that?

Aemon abandoned his chastising of my grandfather and turned to me. "The windows on your new Jeep were busted, but I took care of it."

Dammit.

As sore as I was about the last Jeep I'd lost, I wasn't too keen on having to replace another one. My old Jeep was bright cherry red but had been summarily decimated by a ghoul's fist. The new one was fine enough, but it wasn't the same. Sure, Bishop had never sat in this one—never driven it—but it also meant neither had my dad. I'd take the reminder of Bishop over the loss of another thing my dad had touched.

"Thanks," I whispered before taking a sip of coffee.

Aemon regularly did shit like that. Fixing my windows, saving me from zombies—you know, nice shit. It was so weird. I couldn't tell if he was still trying to make up for possessing me or wanted...

No. Do not go down that path, Darby. There lies danger.

Sloane snorted, but kept her mouth shut. *Thankfully.* If she had her way, she'd needle me about the demon until the end of time.

"You said you had a lead?" I pressed, pouring Aemon a cup of coffee in his favorite mug, and doctoring it like he usually took it—a splash of cream and two sugars.

He loved the blue mug with the tiny chip in the handle, saying it was his favorite color. I had a set of six just like it, but he'd only take the one with the chip.

In the three months since Bishop had fallen off the map, Aemon had been around a lot. Checking in, sniffing out leads he thought were too dangerous for me, random macho bullshit. I was almost used to him coming around.

Almost.

"Yes, I have a contact in Paris that is willing to meet. Says he'll only talk about it in person. I figured you wanted to be in on this, yes?"

A teensy bit of hope bloomed in my gut, which warred with my general uneasiness when it came to Aemon in general.

But it had been three months—*three*—and it was as if Bishop La Roux was a damn ghost. No, he was worse than a ghost. If he were a damn ghost, I could've found the fucker already. But someone not wanting to talk over the phone about him maybe meant they had something substantial. As much as I loved a good case file, they had led to exactly dick.

"Absolutely. When and where?"

Aemon's gaze skated over the other people in the room. "In a few days. Tell me—do you have a passport?"

"Why does she need a passport?" Jay asked, his head still perched on the counter. He was just as used to

Aemon's comings and goings as I was—so much so, he didn't even flinch anymore. Okay, so his vampire-ish tendencies lent him extra warning when the demon was near, but still. "Can't you just zip-zap to France?"

The demon in question sipped his coffee as a dark expression pulled at his usual smile.

"No, I cannot."

"Bu—"

"I'm still a demon, Prince of Hell or not. I can't travel over oceans without taking a trip to the Underworld first." He directed his attention to me. "You pick, Flower. A plane ride or a trip to Hell that saves us eight hours."

The thought of going to the Underworld—and what Sloane had gone through just to get there the first time—made my skin crawl. No, thanks. I liked my toes exactly where they were.

"I have a passport."

I should have taken the trip to the Underworld.

That thought had plagued me since I agreed to this damn adventure. Mainly because I was not a good flyer.

There were too many people in the airport, and what if you didn't get there in time and what if they searched your luggage and decided to confiscate everything? There were far too many variables when it came to air travel, and I was in charge of none of them.

Not. A. Fan.

But when we arrived at the airport, it was not on the super commercial side. When the smoke from Aemon's power faded, we were outside a giant hangar with a few people milling about like little worker bees. An airplane sat just off the tarmac with a red carpet leading to the boarding stairs.

"Umm…" I said nervously, staring at a suit-clad flight attendant who just seemed to notice us standing there.

I had never flown private in my life, but it seemed that streak was about to end.

"Did you honestly think I was going to make you fly commercial?" Aemon scoffed, shaking his head as he pulled his hands away from my hips. "After the Orlando trip? Never."

He was referring to my senior trip when my plane nearly went down after an electrical disturbance. I hadn't flown since, and I was pretty sure I would need pharmaceuticals to do it this time. But there was only one way Aemon knew about my flying trauma because Jay and I refused to talk about it *ever*.

It was the same reason he knew every other corner of my brain. Because he had seen it in my memories when he invaded my mind during his possession.

"What are the odds that flight attendant has Xanax in

his pocket?" I asked, choosing to ignore the reminder of Aemon's possession completely.

He seemed to consider my question as he ushered us forward. "I'd say pretty good, but I wouldn't take them. He'd likely confuse them for the Molly in his other pocket and then you'd really be in trouble."

My feet nearly stuttered to a stop as my tongue felt heavy in my mouth and sweat broke out all over my skin. I did not want to get onto that plane. Not at all.

"Come on, Flower. I'll hold your hand the whole time."

Now I was hot, but it was due to anger rather than anything else. "I'm not a child. I don't need you to hold anything for me."

Choking down my fear, I marched to the plane, handed off my suitcase, and made it up the steps before the fear could take root again.

"You can sit anywhere. Would you like something to drink?" The attendant was my height with a shock of ginger hair and a jaw you could sharpen blades on.

The hum of the engine started, and it took everything in me not to climb out of my skin, holding onto the chaos magic like it was my job. I chose a seat and waved him off.

"I'm fine." I was *not* fine, but I would grit my teeth

and make it so. Closing my eyes, I let my head fall back to the cushion.

Eight hours. Just eight tiny hours and you will be there. You'll get answers. This is fine.

"You're such a little liar," Aemon whispered in my ear, his approach completely undetected.

I cracked an eyelid, cutting my gaze to him with a glare that should have roasted him on the spot.

"You couldn't be less fine if you tried. Now, I can help calm you down, or you can sit there and pray you don't blow this plane up mid-flight. Your choice, Flower."

Aemon had a habit of making me sleep when I needed it. There had been a few instances where I had gone days without even so much as a wink of it until he took the decision out of my hands.

Him actually asking this time was new.

"I could have sworn I had a name, and it wasn't anything even remotely resembling 'Flower' or anything close to it."

Aemon's petulant sigh practically rattled my bones. "Ms. Darby Adler, will you pretty please with sugar on top hold my hand so I may calm you down on this very treacherous flight over an ocean of salt that will surely kill me dead should you explode this plane and dunk me in it?"

That had my breath hitching in my chest as acid

churned in my gut. Exploding this plane had been a real concern, but now? Now I was holding onto the armrests for dear life, and we hadn't left the tarmac yet.

Aemon's face got right in mine so all I could see were those pretty blue eyes and too-full lips.

"You'd better answer me, Flower, or I'll have to think of other ways to distract you."

His words registered, sure, but I was too busy trying to keep hold of the chaos magic roiling under my skin. That same magic that had a habit of responding to my anxiety in ways that were rather incendiary.

"Answer me or I'll kiss you right now."

That startled me out of my panic, but only just a little. Now I was panicking for a whole other reason.

"I'll hold your hand."

His eyes tightened a touch like that was the wrong answer, but he still pried my fingers from the leather armrest and threaded his through them. "Very good."

Almost instantly, some of my nerves eased as heat threaded through every limb.

"May I calm you?"

Confused, I nodded. Wasn't he already?

He settled back into his seat, a tendril of peace hitting me so fast, I breathed a sigh of relief that seemed to go down to my bones. I hadn't felt something this close to happiness since before I could see ghosts. When Dad was still alive. Before my life went to shit. Before I had too much knowledge and no good way to act on it.

And as good as it felt, I fucking hated it.

"I don't like that you can do this to me," I whispered, my gaze drifting to the window. "This is something I want on my own. Not manufactured. Not fake. When the peace goes away, everything will hurt twice as much because I'll know what I'm missing without it."

"Would you like me to take it back?" he murmured, his voice rough as broken glass.

Squeezing his fingers, I gave him a jerky nod. If he was going to take it away, I'd need to ground myself. And yes, I refused to think about what it meant that I was grounding myself with his touch.

"Would you like to sleep?"

No. I wanted my emotions to be my own for once, with no interference or additives. I wanted to be me—however that was.

"No, thanks."

The flight attendant closed the door, made a few announcements, and then it was if we were alone again.

Aemon finally looked at me, his expression guarded as his probing gaze made my belly do this weird dip thing that had to fall in the "uh-oh" column.

"Very well. You know what this means, don't you?"

That peace I felt a minute ago? Gone.

It was replaced by a sneaking suspicion that I knew exactly what this meant and what was coming next. And in the darker, smuttier parts of my brain—the ones I refused to think about or tell a single soul the details of—I secretly wanted him to make good on a threat.

My heart was beating out of my chest for a vastly different reason than before as Aemon slid closer, his face right in mine, his lips so close, I could feel the heat of his skin seeping into me.

And still, I held his hand—even as I registered the plane moving and picking up speed.

"It means, Flower, that I'll have to distract you. Would you like me to distract you?"

My breath hitched as his lips very nearly touched mine.

My body checked out from my brain because I found myself nodding, my nose brushing against his as our lips almost met.

There were a thousand reasons why this was a bad idea. A million. But still, with his body this close to me, and his heat seeping into my bones, and his scent surrounding me? It was really tough to think about any of them.

But he didn't move any closer, and I wanted his lips on mine so much, I was the one that cut the distance between us, capturing that wicked smile for myself. My lips touching his seemed to surprise him for a second, but he rallied not a moment later, threading his free hand in my hair as he banded the other around my back.

Yeah, the peace was gone, but what I felt instead was a whole lot better. His heat was everywhere, like he had turned every bit of the fire under his skin on full blast, tangling his tongue with mine as he took every bit of my control away. Those feelings I'd kept locked down tight? They were bubbling to the surface, and I had half a mind to straddle his lap and...

A clearing of a throat in the distance made me remember that we were not alone on this plane.

Whoops.

Aemon broke the kiss slowly, leisurely, but his hands remained exactly where they were. It was as if he had no intention of letting me slip away from him, no plans whatsoever to let me go.

"Sufficiently distracted, I think. Let me know if you need another one. I'd be more than happy to oblige."

The heat in his gaze told me that if I needed another distraction, whatever he'd use was probably more than I'd bargain for.

3

There was no way my luck was this bad.

Wait, no, scratch that.

Looking back over the last year and a half, it was entirely possible that my luck may have taken a swan dive into shit-town. Had I picked up a bad penny? Angered an ancient witch hell-bent on teaching me a lesson? Or was it just the circumstances of the absolute shitshow I'd made for myself?

Only time would tell.

It still didn't mean I wanted to go anywhere near this place.

"Oh, come on," Aemon murmured in my ear, his smooth voice both sexy as hell and irritating as fuck. "You're the one who wanted to talk to my contact. It just so happens my contact is down here."

I swore, I could've kicked that demon up and down Paris and maybe right into a fucking ocean. The "down here" he was referring to was the catacomb underneath Paris. A catacomb likely full to the damn brim with ghosts. A fucking cave system practically teeming with the dead, and he wanted me to just waltz in there like I owned the place.

Sure.

I was peachy-*fucking*-keen.

It wasn't like I had PTSD from the last time I was in a cave or anything. It wasn't like I hadn't damn near died in a place just like this, surrounded by dead things. It wasn't like I wasn't scared out of my damn mind that somehow Bishop was in that cave already, just waiting for me to steamroll in like I was fucking invincible or something.

But I wasn't invincible. I'd learned that lesson already. Nero's torture and Bishop's betrayal had shown me all I needed to know.

It took everything I had to remember who I was. That I wasn't some naïve little newbie with no power and no allies and no way to defend myself. I was a Daughter of Death. I was a demigod for fuck's sake. I was filled with chaos magic, and if those dead—or Bishop himself—wanted to start something, I could finish it.

I could.

Probably.

And I was so pissed that Aemon of all people would take me here of all places, every single bit of the progress we'd made on the plane had crumbled to dust in my chest. I'd kissed him. *Me.* I'd been the one to reach those last few inches. I'd been the one to press my lips to his. When he gasped in surprise, it had been *me* who swept my tongue into his mouth.

And damn, had that kiss been fucking combustible. Had we been alone, I couldn't be sure what would have happened. But we hadn't been alone, so I'd fallen asleep on that stupid plane ride, resting my head on his shoulder and everything.

Now, I was so mad, I couldn't fathom ever doing it again.

Why in the high holy fuck would he take me here? But unfortunately, there was nothing to be done about it. I was meeting Aemon's contact, and after I did, I was going to punch that damn demon right in the face.

"Your contact had better have something, Aemon, or I swear to everything holy, I will rip him apart with my fucking teeth."

It wasn't like I had another option. It was bad enough we'd exhausted every contact, whisper, and rock to be turned, looking for Bishop in the last three months. Either that asshole had gone to another dimension to hide from me, or he was such an expert at disappearing, he could hide from Death herself. Maybe he'd picked up enough pointers from my bastard of a brother that he could hide until the end of time.

"That's my angry little flower. I was wondering where she went for a second."

There went those butterflies again. *Nope. No. We were mad at him. Mad.*

We were about to go into a damn catacomb because of the last man to compliment me like I was the freaking sun. It had been bullshit then, and even though it was a very different man, it was still bullshit now.

"I'm not your anything, Aemon," I reminded him —*and myself.* "I'm not your flower, your love, or your responsibility." And it didn't matter how good it felt that he was here practically holding my hand, that didn't mean I'd be falling for anyone's shit. Ever. Again.

Aemon checked his watch. "Right on time. It's only been ten hours since you reminded me you were a big girl who could do this by yourself, and you don't need me tagging along. Do you think if you keep saying it, it'll sink in or—"

Growling, I stalked toward the entrance, leaving the Prince of Hell behind. There were plenty of reasons to hate Aemon. He was too damn pretty, for one. Then there was that whole 'possessing me' thing. There were plenty of reasons not to trust Aemon, too.

It had been my father who locked him up for two thousand years.

It had been my father who punished him.

And it didn't matter if he made me feel like a cherished piece of crystal in his hands or how many times he'd pulled my ass out of the flames. Or how fucking searingly perfect his kiss had been.

It didn't. *I swear.*

Because every time I thought about kissing Aemon or maybe having something more, all that filled my brain was how badly I'd misjudged Bishop. How I fit him into my life, how I pinned my hopes on him, how I trusted him with everything and then found out every bit of it had been fake.

That he'd used me.

That he was just a plant.

That he'd manipulated everything.

My feet stuttered to a stop as the cold chill of the tunnel system filled my very bones. A wave of souls called to me, singing the song of the dead that I would recognize forever. The very ground beneath my feet buzzed with their energy.

It was one thing to go into a graveyard. It was quite

another to walk through a city-sized tunnel system filled with the dead.

The Paris catacombs had always been at the tippy top of my list of "oh, fuck no" places to go to since I could comprehend what it was. And my imaginings as a teen in my world history class had nothing on this.

My knees wobbled as the weight of all the souls landed on my shoulders. There was no way I would be able to make it in here. Not and stay conscious.

A warm arm wrapped around my waist as Aemon guided us forward, stealing some of the pressure from roughly millions of souls. Sure, I had Shiloh's chaos just running rampant through my veins, but that didn't stop an entire city's worth of dead from stealing my very breath, from stealing every shred of energy, every thought in my head.

"I shouldn't have brought you here," he murmured into my hair, the heat of him making me sway closer, steal more of it. Because it didn't matter how humid or stagnant the air was, I was freezing all the way down to my toes. "Chaos or no, the grave talker bits win out, don't they? The souls. It's too much."

Swallowing, I shook my head. I could make it. *Maybe.* "I—"

His grip tightened on my waist, the tips of his fingers digging into my flesh in a way that wasn't bruising but let me know he wasn't taking any of my bullshit.

"I swear to Hades himself, if you say you're fine, I will turn you over my knee and spank that fabulous arse of yours."

It was tough to say if I wanted to test him, zip my mouth shut, or do a whole-body shiver because *damn.* That sentence was enough to cut through every ache in my body and burrow down deep into my middle. I totally should *not* be turned on by that, right? Because if his kisses could steal all my worry, what would happen if I just let him...

You're here to do a job, Darby. Remember the last guy that distracted you like this?

That sobered me right up.

"I'm not fine." Fine waved bye-bye ages ago. I couldn't be sure if I'd *ever* been fine. If Aemon's peace magic told me anything, I was a ball of internalized rage and two steps away from flipping everyone off as I jumped off the ledge. I was so far from fine, I had half a mind to check myself into a facility and just stay there. "I was going to tell you that I'd manage if it meant we caught this fucker."

Aemon grumbled but kept walking us forward. "You'll manage? Sure. You'll manage your way straight into a grave if you're not careful."

I'd have quipped back something smart, but as many times as he'd pulled my ass from the brink, I didn't have a leg to stand on in that fight. Plus, the mouth of the tunnel system swallowed us up, the bone-filled walls telling the tale of more death than my brain could comprehend. Once upon a time, I had been a host for thousands of souls—hundreds of thousands—and still, this was so much more, so much bigger.

The scent of old death filled my nose as the humid air closed in around us.

But something about the catacombs felt different than any other place for the dead. This was bigger than any graveyard, any totem of souls, any cemetery. And it wasn't just the dead. Souls might have lined the walls of the tunnel, but the energy here was just... *off*.

"What the fuck is that?" I whispered, a chill sweeping down my spine as I tried to not make eye contact with any ghost—tough to do since the place was swarming with them.

Aemon's hold tightened on my waist. "Later, Flower. Let's get in and out of here before this place decides to keep us, yes?"

"What did I say about calling me that?"

He let out a dark chuckle. "Oh, I heard you. I'm just choosing to ignore it."

Aemon led me farther into the tunnel system, my

gaze trained on the ground and nowhere else. All it would take was one of those ghosts to make eye contact and then it was all over. I'd get swarmed and keel over from the weight of them all.

Or rather, explode, but that would be splitting hairs.

But the farther we walked—okay, it was Aemon practically carrying me—into the tunnel, the more crammed it got. Specters were everywhere I looked, filling every millimeter of space until there was nothing I could do but let their ghostly chill freeze me from the inside out.

The whispers came as soon as a specter touched me. *Grave talker.* Soon, they weren't just standing there. They were talking to each other, the hiss of my particular brand of arcane passing through the crowd like a swarm of bees.

Fuck.

A young boy shoved through the legs of the crowd, latching onto my arm with a grip that burned me from the inside out. He begged me in his native tongue to take him to see his mother, his tattered clothes and dirty face making it almost impossible to place when he'd died.

But I couldn't take anyone.

Because if I took one, I'd have to take them all. All of them would want to move on, and then...

And then I'd be in real trouble.

A swarm of darkness filled my vision, as Aemon let out a guttural growl. It seemed like the Prince of Hell at my side had decided I was done trying to handle the situation on my own. Vicious French fell from his lips, a warning I only understood on the periphery as I struggled to breathe. My French was rusty, sure, but it didn't matter.

It was like I was getting swarmed by those wolves again. All of them touching me, clawing at me, tearing me apart in that cave. My breath stuttered in my lungs as my heart threatened to beat out of my chest.

No. Not again. Please.

It didn't matter that the specters were moving away from me or that Aemon had me held close to his chest or that our path was now clear. That fear had taken root, twining so deep in my soul, I thought I would never get free.

The ground beneath my feet rumbled, threatening to cave the whole place in on our heads.

No, please. Please don't let me die in here. Get me out. Getmeoutgetmeoutgetmeout.

Then I wasn't in that fucking cave anymore. Light flooded my senses as cool air filled my nose. Cobblestones bit into my palms as I sucked in that beautiful, non-humid, non-death scented, fresh oxygen, letting it cleanse the panic.

"Fucking hell, Flower. Did you just travel on your own?" Aemon's hand rubbed the center of my back while I tried to stuff my panic down where it damn well belonged.

But I couldn't look at him. I couldn't do anything but breathe and pray I never went in that fucking tunnel ever again. Still, I was too close to the place.

Something about it made me think of the boogeyman under a bed, ready to grab your ankles at any second and drag you under.

Staggering to standing, I kept my gaze forward and started walking. I didn't give a shit what Aemon's contact had to say.

I wasn't going back in that cave.

Not ever.

4

The fridge in the villa was twice the size of the one I had in my own kitchen. And yes, Aemon had rented or bought or knew a guy, and we were staying in an honest-to-god villa in Versailles about a stone's throw from the palace proper. Everything about it was completely gorgeous and infuriating all at the same time.

The bedrooms were fit for royalty, the architecture was divine, *blah*, *blah*, *blah*. I didn't see any of it. I was too pissed.

How could he have taken me there? Didn't he know just how scared I was of cemeteries and graveyards, and any other place that was dark and filled with the dead? Didn't he know how the dead had consumed every part of my life until Hildy came and helped me push them out? Didn't he know how they drained every bit of me? How they'd stolen my sanity, my energy, my peace?

Aemon knew everything else. Why didn't he know that?

I let the cool air wash over my body as I contemplated my next meal. I had already blown through an entire chicken, a whole baguette longer than my arm, a platter of cheese and fruit, and I was still hungry. A million-plus ghosts were down in that fucking tunnel and they leeched every bit of energy from my bones. I wouldn't feel anything close to human until I had more coffee, a bottle of vodka, another baguette, and three days of sleep.

Too bad I had to settle for only the baguette.

Footsteps approached, but I paid them no attention. Maybe Aemon would take the hint.

"Flower—"

Or maybe not.

I slammed the fridge door closed, unable to even look at him. How could he take me to that fucking tunnel? It wasn't like I'd been by myself when Bishop rose the dead to attack me. Aemon had been there. He'd healed me. He brought me back from the brink of death himself and he thought...

"Darby, please look at me."

But I couldn't. It was as if every bad thought in my head was true. That he didn't care. That he wanted to punish me for what my father had done. That he was no better than Bishop or Essex or Mariana.

That he was using me.

And that hurt so fucking bad I felt like I couldn't breathe. Because... I didn't want to think about that *because*. It would break me. I just knew it.

A soft hand curled around my elbow, but as kind as the touch was, as much as I craved it, all it did was set me off.

I whirled, yanking my arm out of his hold. "Did you think that was funny?" I spat, channeling my rage at the source of my pain. "Sending me down there? Goading me. Did you get a kick out of me losing my shit? Did it make you feel like a *big man*?"

My entire body flashed with heat as fury took over. The stove clicked on, gas flames shooting up from the burners. Aemon's gaze fell to them, but he moved on like they were nothing, choosing to step closer, come closer...

Didn't he know that he shouldn't? Didn't he know that I was dangerous? Why didn't he see that I was so close to losing it? Why didn't he care?

"No, Darby. I would never do that to you. I thought you were trying to conquer what had happened to you. I thought—" He shook his head, fake remorse and fake concern and fake—it was all fake. "Had I known you would react that way, I would never have taken you there."

Liar.

The pots hanging above the stove clanged together, shimmying like they were dying to fly from their hooks and bean him in the head. Or maybe *I* wanted to bean him in the head.

"Sure, Aemon. Totally plausible, except you were there." I tried to swallow down every bit of the fear, the hurt, but it seemed lodged in my throat. "You saw everything that happened to me in that cave and you... You knew how scared I was—"

I struggled to breathe again. It hurt so fucking bad. A thousand times worse than when Bishop betrayed me. Did I just care about Aemon more? Or was it like cutting over a scar, the pain doubled the second time?

"How about I lock you in a coffin and see how you react? How about I dump you in a hole and leave you to rot? How'd that be?"

My questions were cruel, but he needed to see that they were the same. Aemon had been locked away, too. He knew how devastating it was to feel trapped. Betrayed. He knew the dirty feeling of losing trust in someone you loved.

He. Knew.

"No—"

The water turned on by itself as the lights flickered and the windows rattled. The cabinet doors swung on their hinges, slamming back and forth like they were trying to take flight. "How am I supposed to trust you, Aemon? How?"

That had him falling back on a foot like I'd shoved him or something. "I have never given you a reason not to trust me. I—"

The laugh that came out of me was mirthless. "My father locked you up for two thousand years. I don't know how old you are, but I have a feeling that wasn't exactly a picnic. But he's dead. You can't get back at a dead man, but you can take out your revenge on his children."

A knowing expression fell over his face. "After everything I've done, after every time I have come to you when you needed me, you're still waiting on me to turn on you, aren't you?" He moved closer, trying to touch me, but I circled the island, putting it between us.

Aemon nodded to himself. "You think what your father did was wrong. You think my punishment was too harsh. But it was my own father that did it to me, yours was just the instrument. If I were to get back at anyone, it wouldn't be you. It would never be you or yours."

Black smoke filled the room for a single moment, and

then Aemon reformed right next to me, towering over me like he really wanted me to hear him.

"And when I find Bishop La Roux, I will personally hold him still while you cut off his head. Because had he not fucked with your brain and your heart, I wouldn't have to work so fucking hard to get you to see sense. In case the kiss on the plane wasn't clear, I care about you, Darby. A lot."

As good as that statement felt, I didn't trust it for a second. I didn't trust Aemon's open face or the way my body felt being so close to him. I didn't trust anything— especially how my body reacted to his.

"I'm supposed to believe you saw inside my head, poked around all my memories, and somehow you still want to be with me? That you like me. Did your time in a box make you batshit insane or are you just dense? No one in their right mind would want me after that."

A faint smile lifted the edges of his mouth. "My time-out was not as difficult to endure as you might think. Yes, I wanted out of that box, but I'm not traumatized by it. I am ancient, Darby. When you think of time, it is in years, decades. When I think of time, it is in eons. My father sent me to my room, and as soon as I saw a chance to get free, I took it. It was only after seeing your heart, your mind, did I feel remorse for what I had done."

And all the while he came closer, boxing me in, crowding me. "Am I in my right mind? Maybe not, but I liked what I saw in yours. I liked your drive and loyalty and fire. Your willingness to do what needed to get done. Your love of your family. The way your mind works. There are things I hate, too, but anyone who cares about you would hate them, too."

My butt hit the edge of the counter, stopping my retreat, and Aemon rested a hand on the stone, bracketing my hips so there was no chance of me getting away. I wasn't exactly sure I wanted to.

"So tell me, Flower—are you going to admit you feel something for me, too, or do I need to do a little more convincing?"

Swallowing hard, I asked the question—the real one —that had been plaguing me since he put me to sleep the first time in the car what felt like ages ago. "You can manipulate me—calm me down, make me sleep." I grabbed the necklace that protected my mind from Bishop. "How do I know you aren't making me feel like this? How do I know if it's real? How do I know—"

Aemon's gaze flashed with the fire of his demon as black smoke billowed through the room. "I am not Bishop La Roux. I cannot do you harm even if I wanted to. I can only put you to sleep because you wish it. I can only give you peace because you crave it. I am a demon,

Darby, but demons can only manipulate what is already inside a person."

And as mad as he was, somehow, I still wasn't scared.

"You want me. You want to trust me. You want to fall for me. You just won't let yourself believe it. Because every person you have ever let go with has failed you."

That pissed me off. "Get out of my head."

He pressed his body against mine, a wicked smile blooming over his lips. "I'm not in your head, Flower." He tapped on my sternum. "I'm in here. I know what you really want. I can practically taste it. The question is—are you going to let me give it to you?"

I had never been so happy for padded bras in my life because my nipples could probably cut glass. And that said nothing about the way my breath stuttered in my lungs and my thighs clenched.

"That depends," I breathed, hoping I sounded coy or even a little sexy.

Aemon seemed to press into me more, filling the minute space with every fiber of himself. His scent invaded my nose, his heat filtered through my body. He was everywhere, in everything. And as much as I wanted to not trust him, as much as I wanted to hold onto the ghost of my failures, I didn't have a leg to stand on.

"On what?"

"On if I am here, too." I tapped on his chest, my

fingers lingering, as if taking them away was tantamount to torture.

How did I get here? How had I gone from wanting to murder him to wanting him so badly, I was fighting with myself to not rise on my toes and just kiss him?

Because you've always been fighting.

Because you know he's different.

Because somewhere inside you, you know he has only ever protected you.

Aemon's smile practically curled my toes. His hand covered mine on his chest, pressing it into his skin like he wanted my hold to never leave him.

"As if you don't know already."

He cupped my face, jerking my jaw up and exposing my mouth to his. But he didn't kiss me. No, he hovered, he waited, drawing out this tension in my gut until it snapped.

Until I snapped.

Unable to stop myself, I gave in and reached up on my toes, pressing a fevered kiss to his lips, tasting him. Again, it took him a second to respond, his surprise doing funny things to my belly. Oh, but when he did, it was as if I had given him the green light on every dirty fantasy I refused to admit to.

One second, I was standing there wedged against the counter, his body pressed against mine, and the next?

He'd lifted me in his arms, swiveled around, and planted my ass on the counter, his slim hips between my legs as he devoured my mouth.

The windows rattled and the pots clanked, and the gas stove had a stroke, but I didn't give a shit. I was too preoccupied with Aemon's thumb grazing the underside of my breast, his other hand holding onto my ass like it was a damn life raft, and his mouth moving from mine to my neck.

A hint of fang grazed my skin, and I was a goner.

Ten minutes ago, I was ready to kill Aemon. Now? I was ripping his shirt from his skin and struggling with the buckle of his belt.

Maybe I could fuck him out of my system. Maybe I could let myself trust him just this once. Maybe I could breathe him in and let him do whatever he wanted to me and then let him go before I got too attached.

The lusty part of my brain was totally on board with this.

But the smart part?

She really fucking doubted it.

5

"Tell me what you want, Flower," Aemon whispered against my neck, letting his lips, his fangs graze the skin as he spoke.

But I didn't know what I wanted. The possibilities were endless. He could do damn near anything to me and I'd likely love every fucking minute of it. I especially wanted him to keep doing that thing with his hand on my ribs and his thumb almost grazing my nipple. Every time I moaned, his fingers tightened, and it let me know he was into this just as much as I was.

His hand went to my ponytail, and he yanked at the elastic, letting my hair free. Weaving his fingers through it, he tugged, exposing my throat even more to his mouth. Belt forgotten, I let him nibble and suck and wind me up so tight.

It was glorious.

Then his mouth was on mine again, but this time, he didn't kiss me.

"Tell me what you want, Flower," Aemon repeated, his voice a guttural growl that reminded me he, indeed, was a demon from the very depths of Hell. At the moment, I couldn't find a single thing wrong with that, either. "Tell me how you wish me to please you."

But I didn't want to answer him. Him asking reminded me of a man I never wanted to think about again—especially not right now.

"Don't ask," I whispered against his lips. "I don't care what you do, just don't ask. Take me, possess me, fuck me, worship me. Just don't ask me. Please?"

"Darby, I don—"

"He manipulated everything," I hissed, cutting him off, failing to meet his gaze. "He asked me questions and then pulled the strings to get the answers he wanted."

Aemon's eyes tightened as his irises flashed with the fire of Hell itself. His body seemed to grow bigger, melting into the smoke of his demon form. But instead of feeling scared, I just felt protected. Safe. Like he'd rain down every bit of his power on those that would do me harm.

"I want this with you, but if you treat me like I'm a broken thing, I can't—"

Aemon tightened his fist in my hair, pulling my head back and exposing my neck. "You are the most beautiful woman I have ever seen," he murmured, his lips grazing my throat as he spoke. "Every time I look at you—your strength, your fire—I want to pin you against the closest wall and fuck you until neither of us can stand up. I want to cart you off to some deserted island where there's nothing but sand and sex and food until you lose that haunted look in your eyes. And I don't give a sodding fuck what I have to burn to make it happen, either."

Fangs nipped at my bottom lip—the sting so good I thought I was going to pass out.

"You want me to take, Flower? I'll take. Just know that even when I'm through, I won't be giving you back. Understand? You're mine. Thorns and all."

He readjusted his grip, pulling me so close it was as if he were melding me into his skin. "Do you hear me? You're mine. *Mine.*"

Maybe it was the trauma speaking or maybe it was the chaos magic still coursing through my veins. Maybe it was a baser need, I didn't know. But I knew what response I'd get when I said what was dying to fall out of my mouth.

"Prove it."

Did I just throw down the mother of all dares to a Prince of Hell?

Yes, I indeed did do something of the sort, yes.

Was I sorry?

Absolutely fucking not.

A single raised eyebrow had my sex clenching and my breaths coming in labored pants. A snap of his fingers later, and I was naked in his arms, my bare skin brushing against the soft luxurious fabric of his suit.

"Hold onto something, Flower," he commanded, removing my fingers from his belt and placing them on the counter.

A second later, he had ahold of my ass, and was dragging it to the edge of the stone. Then those long, sexy fingers went to the knot in his tie, loosening it before he spread my legs wide and got down to the business of devouring me.

And devour me, he did.

I quickly realized why he had told me to hang on, because as soon as his breath hit my sex, it was as if a thousand touches had lit my nerve endings on fire. Heat and power raced over my body as if the dense smoke filling the room was just an extension of him, plucking at my nipples, licking up my spine, biting at my neck, and with Aemon's tongue at my center…

I held on for dear life as he licked me, sucked me, and ate me up like I was his favorite meal. Not a single millimeter of my skin remained untouched by his mouth, and when his lips closed over that sensitive bundle of nerves, I came undone.

The counter cracked beneath my fingers, the last vestige that held me back crumbling to dust in my hands. Then I couldn't stop my hips from rocking into his mouth or the moans erupting from my throat or my hands going into his hair.

"That's it, Flower. Let me hear you."

Shamelessly, I sought out my pleasure, letting the chaos and the freedom and the desire course through me. It was as if his touch was everywhere, his heat, his fire, and when his fingers slipped inside me, I was lost, detonating like a damn bomb.

Lights flickered, glass cracked, fire bloomed from the stove, and I couldn't make myself give a shit about any of it. Because as good as I felt, I had somehow become a junkie—an Aemon junkie.

I needed more. I needed everything. I needed him.

"More," I rasped when I could string my motor functions together enough to speak. "I want more."

Those fire eyes seemed to melt me to the counter as a wicked grin slowly pulled at Aemon's lips.

"Oh, Flower," he tutted, lifting me off the counter and into his arms. "I'm just getting started."

A second later, my back hit a mattress, but I didn't even see the room before I had ahold of Aemon's tie, yanking his mouth to mine. I wished I knew what spell he'd used to get my clothes off so fast because I wanted his skin on mine so bad I could taste it.

No, I *couldn't* taste it, and that was the problem.

No sooner had the desire passed through my brain did Aemon back away, ripping his tie off his neck. He shrugged out of his suit jacket and oh, so slowly unbuttoned his crisp black shirt, revealing golden skin inch by inch. He peeled his shirt off, and something in me yanked him closer.

Call it chaos or just my baser needs, but I just couldn't care. His warm skin was on mine and his lips were on mine and my hands were roaming every inch I could reach. We rolled, him letting me take the top as I struggled to get his pants undone. A moment later, I'd reached the end of my patience, ripping his suit and underwear until there was nothing between us.

Delicious heat seared through me as a growl rumbled from his chest, his eyes rolling back into his head as his hands gripped my hips and held me still. Somehow, I got the feeling that he was the one holding himself back.

"I thought I told you to take, Aemon," I murmured coyly as I swiveled my hips. "Why are you holding yourself back from me?"

He sat up, nipping at my bottom lip as he

contemplated his answer. "You won't ever be rid of me if we do this, you know that, right?"

I was willing to take my chances. In all likelihood, he would leave when he got his fill. That could be in two hours or ten years. I wasn't stupid enough to think Aemon and I were forever.

All I did was smile as I rolled my hips. "Do your worst."

His arm banded around my back, pulling me against his chest as his other hand threaded through my hair. The gentle pull at my scalp became insistent.

"My worst, Flower?" he growled against my neck, his fangs nipping but not breaking the skin. "You sure?" Smoke billowed through the room as his eyes blazed from blue to the fire of his demon, and damn, if I didn't like that better.

Gods, his heat was like finally thawing after a cold winter. The ice around my heart seemed to melt. I bit my lip, rocking my hips to try and get him inside me.

I needed him inside me.

"I want this. Stop teasi—"

But my words were cut off by his lips on mine and his cock filling me to the hilt in one long, slow stroke. If I thought I felt heat before, it was nothing on the inferno that threaded through my limbs then. I could barely breathe I was so full, and when he pulled out, I actually whimpered at the loss.

We rolled again, Aemon pressing me into the bed before he hooked his arms around my thighs, yanking me down on his cock. His hands bracketed my waist, holding me still as he fucked me like the demon he was. And he did have to hold me still because I was writhing, my back arching off the bed as he thrust into me with the single-minded focus of a man refusing to take prisoners.

"Look at you taking me so well. You're fucking beautiful like this, Flower."

When my orgasm nearly reached me, Aemon pulled out, flipped me over and slammed back into me, one arm banding around my chest as the other tilted my head so he could own me with a searing kiss.

But if he thought my orgasm was a safe distance away, he was sorely mistaken.

If anything, the new position made it come faster, harder, blazing through me like a damn comet. And when it hit, all I could do was hold onto Aemon for dear life, praying there would be something left of me when this was all over.

"Are you hungry?" Aemon asked in between nibbles on my shoulder. He never broke my skin, but I could tell he wanted to really bad. A part of me wondered if his bites were drugging and what they could do to someone like me. The other part craved them all over me and damn the consequences.

In the last twenty-four hours—give or take—Aemon and I had mind-bending sex, snacks, and enough orgasms to power the fucking sun.

What we hadn't had was a real meal.

My stomach answered for him, rumbling the whale song of an empty tummy.

"I could eat. Do we have any groceries left?"

He gave me a boyish smile as he shook his head. "No, but I was thinking I could take you out on the town. After the shite plane ride and the disaster at the catacombs, I feel I may have tainted France for you forever."

Considering we were fresh from the shower, and in that shower, he'd given me no less than three orgasms, I highly doubted France was ruined in the slightest, but whatever.

"And you want to take me out to experience French food?" I sat up, ready to get to the meat of what he was asking. "Are you asking me on a date?"

Aemon blinked, his face falling a little, his smile dimming, and I realized I'd asked him like a cop instead of like the woman in his bed.

"Wouldn't dream of it," he whispered, sliding from the sheets as he yanked on a pair of pants.

Oh. Oh, no. It was more than that. I couldn't put my finger on why exactly he was hurt, but...

"I meant, I don't have anything to wear on a date. All I brought were jeans and T-shirts. If you're taking me on a real date, I'll need something special."

Smiling, I stood from the bed, visualizing what I wanted. I needed a dress so sexy he'd have to fight with himself to not fuck me in public. When I had it, I snapped my fingers, hoping the chaos magic didn't do me wrong.

Stealing a peek, a smile stretched my mouth wide. It had been a long time since I had even wanted to wear a dress, but the scarlet-red backless number I had on was smooth as butter and made my legs look about a mile long. And the look on Aemon's face?

Totally worth it. His pants were left hanging loose on his hips, all but forgotten, as his blue eyes blazed with fire. His chest heaved with a long intake of air as his nostrils flared.

"Fuck the restaurant," he murmured, dematerializing from across the room and appearing right in front of me.

"Oh, no." I giggled, dodging his hold. "You can't dangle food in front of me and then take it away. I require sustenance if I want to survive whatever it is you've got going on inside your head."

A snap later and my hair and makeup were good to go, and if the mirror were to be believed, it wasn't too bad. The glam waves and subtle makeup were done up without being overdone.

Rising up on my strappy heels, I nibbled at Aemon's lip.

"Feed me, handsome. I'm starving."

6

The restaurant was buzzing with conversation as Aemon and I strode toward our table behind the tiny waiter. Tucked in a secluded corner behind a wall of wine, I slid onto the royal-blue upholstered chair. Instead of Aemon letting the small man try and help me scoot in my seat, he took over, dropping a kiss to the back of my neck before he left me to take his own.

He didn't sit across from me, either. No, he sat right next to me, picking up my hand and bringing it to his mouth, a hint of fang scraping my skin as he dropped a kiss to the inside of my wrist.

Holy. Shit.

I couldn't remember my last date.

No, I *could*, but I was choosing not to at the moment.

No one needed to think about the guy who thought honking outside my house instead of coming to my door equated a good way to start the night. Nor did I need to dwell on the fact he wanted *me* to pay for the both of us, commented on everything I ate, and told me I should probably slow down on the desserts because I needed to lose a few pounds.

There was a reason I hadn't had a boyfriend in five years before Bishop showed up.

And look how well that turned out.

But this... This was different.

Not only did Aemon look like he'd just walked right out of a magazine in his black suit, black shirt, and black tie, but the way his hair was pushed back from his face and the way he looked at me like if he didn't hold himself back, he'd fuck me on the floor of this joint?

Yeah, it did things to me. Sexy, dirty things that had me pressing my knees together to stave off the ache in my sex.

The waiter spoke in rapid French, going over the specials as I struggled to keep up. I had a small knowledge of the language but wasn't very good at it. Aemon answered him, the words flowing from his mouth like a ribbon of silk.

Okay, it shouldn't be that hot, right? Just being in

command of a situation and knowing another language should be commonplace and no big deal.

But damn if I didn't want to kiss him in the middle of this restaurant. And yes, I should totally do that language matrixing spell that Sloane had suggested before we left.

Later.

It damn well would have to be later because Aemon slowly pulled my chair closer to his so he could whisper in my ear.

"Steak, duck, or the chicken?" There was no reason on this green earth why his voice should damn near give me an orgasm, but here we were.

Food, Darby. You need food so you can keep up with his sexy ass.

"Steak. Medium. And potatoes—I don't care how they come—all potatoes are valid."

Aemon's smile widened. "And enough bread to soak up the Seine, all the desserts, and you're going to want at least five bites off my plate, so I had better make it good, right?"

Fiery heat crept into my cheeks as I pressed my lips together into a sheepish smile. "You are correct."

"Very well, scallops or chicken?"

I may have melted right there on the spot.

No one in the history of ever had just *known* that I was essentially one step away from the Cookie Monster when it came to food and needed all of it or I'd be a raging bitch. Sure, I realized why Aemon knew this information, but that mattered less and less the more he actually utilized it to make me happy.

There were plenty of times I'd practically gift wrapped the cheat codes to a guy only to have him toss them in the trash. Aemon may have snooped inside my brain, but damn, if he hadn't learned all he needed to while he was there.

"Scallops. I heard the word truffle in there somewhere, right?"

His pleased smile told me that's the one he wanted, too, and if he didn't quit being so hot, I was going to melt into the floor.

He completed the order, handed off our menus, and settled into his seat, all the while never letting go of my hand. He'd been like that the whole day and all of last night—always within touching distance, always brushing my hand or holding me close. It was as though any second, he was expecting me to run away screaming.

Either that, or he got the same damn high I did when our skin made contact.

"Did you know you blush so fucking pretty when I kiss your wrist?" he asked, and I fought off the urge to drag him to the nearest quiet corner and let him...

"Did you know if you keep asking me things like that

I'm going to combust right here and right now? It's always the torture with you demons, isn't it?"

He gave me an unrepentant grin. "Admit it, you like my torture."

A movie of the greatest hits from the last twenty-four hours played in my head. *Oh, yeah*. I loved his brand of torture.

"Very well," he said on a sigh. "Tell me what your childhood was like."

Shrugging, I sat back in my chair. "Why? You know everything already."

His lips twisted in chagrin as he played with my fingers, but still, he pressed. "Because context is everything, and I want to know more. Because you could tell me the same story a thousand times and I'd never tire of it. Because when it comes to knowing you, I endeavor to be an expert."

It was human nature to want to be known, right? To be seen. But that was a mistake I'd made before—too busy being seen, that I hadn't done any seeing of my own.

"How about you tell me something about your childhood, and I'll do the same?"

"The investigator in you is chomping at the bit, I see?" He shot me a perilously sexy grin. "Very well, though my childhood was an exceedingly long time ago.

Let's see... I once tricked Zephyr into eating a bush from Persephone's Garden and he got stuck in his dragon form for a year as punishment."

He had to be pulling my leg.

"Then again, he had flambéed my favorite sculpture, so I was not sorry in the least."

We went back and forth, trading stories until our food arrived, the meal consisting of enough plates to fill our entire table. And yes, I shared. I also may have threatened Aemon with the most painful of deaths should he tell anyone that I sacrificed food for him, too.

We were in the middle of my favorite dessert of all time when I felt the familiar buzz of an insistent soul desperate for my attention. Grumbling, I tried to ignore him as I stuffed more lemon-raspberry frangipane into my mouth.

Couldn't he see I was on the best date I had ever been on in my life?

Couldn't he tell I was *busy*?

"Allo, miss? Miss Darby Adler?" the ghost asked in heavily accented English. I really needed to do that damn language spell, maybe then I could tell him to fuck off in his native tongue. "Please. My master wishes for me to speak with you?"

Sighing, I shot the specter a disgruntled glare as I finished my dessert. I had no desire to look like a crazy person in the middle of this damn restaurant, so I signaled for him to take a seat.

He was ruining my night, dammit, and I had plans for this dress. Dirty, semi-public, freaky AF plans.

"How can I help you and your *master*?" This close? I knew enough about the man that I didn't really want to get the full story, but ghosts had a way of following me around until I caved, so it was best that I hear him out.

"Master Edoril wishes to speak with you. He says that he will meet you at the entrance to his home since you had trouble traversing the path. Had he known he was meeting with someone such as yourself, he would have suggested another venue."

Aemon's grip tightened on my free hand, the power that usually settled around his shoulders like a shroud practically vibrating with unspent rage.

"Tell your master that *we* have no need to see him. Not after I specifically asked about the state of the place and he outright lied about it," Aemon growled, his eyes flashing with fire for just a moment before he regained his cool. "Edoril can speak to *me*, or he can fuck off."

Aemon was practically seething, and I supposed I could venture a guess as to why. He didn't like things that hurt me, and he especially did not like things that made me not trust him. Whoever this Edoril was, he was fucked as soon as Aemon got a piece of him and not in the good way.

Maybe it was the chaos in me, maybe it was just me, but I *really* wanted to see that.

"The real question is whether or not he has information for us. I'm not too keen on meeting the guy who got me cornered in a death tunnel on purpose any more than you are, but if it means catching—"

"The sooner we cut that bastard's head off, the sooner you stop doing overtly dangerous shit in an effort to kill him. Yes, yes. That is the reason we're here, isn't it?"

Could he honestly blame me? "And you haven't killed people for far less?"

Grumbling, he sat back in his chair again. "I find it supremely unhelpful when you're right."

And even though that damn ghost was sapping my energy, and even though I did not in *any* way want to tread within a mile radius of those catacombs, I still laughed at Aemon's boyish petulance.

"We'll meet with your master..." My power supplied the specter's name. "Claude. You are free to tell him that we will be along shortly." I elbowed Aemon, shooting him a censuring glare that said to be nice.

"Fine, fine. Yes, do tell him. Apologies for my rudeness. I shouldn't shoot the messenger and all that."

Claude seemed to deflate a little in relief, but me? It was the absolute last thing I felt.

When I decided to wear these shoes, I had not taken the act of walking into account. Pretty much every single street was paved in cobblestones or odd-shaped pavers, and the damn things were dangerous for someone not used to wearing heels. I was leaning onto Aemon heavily.

Plus, I hadn't taken into account I was sans underwear while wearing the shortest fucking dress known to mankind. Seriously, there were napkins longer than this thing. Gods forbid I stumbled and fell ass over teakettle. All of Paris would see my lady bits. That was *so* not happening. *Not today, Devil. Not to-day.* Wait, there was a pun... *Never mind. Focus, Darby.*

"I need pants for this," I hissed in Aemon's ear, stumbling yet again on the extremely pretty but treacherous-as-fuck sidewalk.

And weapons.

Weapons wouldn't be a bad idea. I had a very nice iron knife in my bag for just such an occasion. The Fae in the States were spotty at best. Sure, there were cities just dripping with them, but Knoxville wasn't one of them. Savannah had a large population, but from what I'd heard, they usually stuck to the East Coast.

Europe was a whole other animal.

There were more arcaners here than any other part of the world—again, from what I'd heard from Ingrid and Thomas. I had a feeling they'd been out of the loop for a while, but I wasn't about to tell them that. I had a gut feeling there was a decent number of arcaners everywhere, it was just some places kept it more hidden than most.

"Why do you think you need pants for a perfectly peaceful meeting with a contact?" Aemon asked, his eyebrow arched in a way that made me think he knew something I didn't.

To ruin the surprise or not ruin the surprise?

Well, it didn't seem like semi-public wall sex would be in my future now. *Dammit.*

"I'm not wearing any underwear," I said under my breath, almost hoping he wouldn't hear me.

When he tugged me to a stop, I had a feeling that hope was dashed.

I soon found myself in a secluded alcove behind the fronds of several trees as the city seemed to pass us by. My ass met the wall of a building as Aemon hulked over me like a beast. It was fucking delicious.

"What did you just say?"

His growling question had me aching to wrap my legs around him. If I thought the look back at the villa was hot, it had nothing on the one he was giving me now.

"Umm…"

"Please tell me I haven't been sitting right next to your beautifully bare kitten and not known it." His hands reached for the hem of my dress. "Did you do it on purpose, Flower? Is it because you want me with my head between your thighs? Or would you rather I just fuck you against this wall?"

While that was very, *very* tempting—*seriously, so tempting*—I had a feeling Aemon's Fae contact wasn't the patient kind.

"How about pants now, then meet, then wall sex?"

You would have thought I canceled Christmas.

"But—" His fingers tightened on the hem. "What if I just take care of you now and then pants, meet, wall sex?"

We'd figured out in the last twenty-four hours that as much as I enjoyed everything he did in bed, I preferred orgasms that involved his cock inside me. And once I got that, the meeting would not be happening at all.

"Meet first."

"You're no fun, Flower. Not even a taste?" He gave me a full-on pout. "Fine, if you need knickers so bad, but I'm taking this course of action as a promise, you know."

Oh, I knew, and damn if I wouldn't let him when the time came.

I just had to get through this meeting first.

7

I'd never been so happy to be wearing jeans in my life.

Granted, I would have preferred fighting leathers strapped down with an arsenal, but I'd take jeans, Chuck's, and a leather jacket over that scrap of a dress. Aemon was less happy about my choice of garb than I was, but he'd get a present later that would make up for it.

"Tell me about Edoril again?"

Considering Aemon had glossed over the details before our first visit, what I really wanted was the whole truth. That said, I'd take the Cliff's Notes since we were running out of time.

"Not much to know. He's a Bone Fae. No, scratch that —he's *the* Bone Fae. I'm not sure how much you know about them, but I'll give you the gist. The reason there aren't many Bone Fae left? As a species, they are on the more barbaric side, preferring to eat their young rather than raise them. I suppose when dying of old age isn't a real concern, population replacement goes out the window."

And we were just walking in there? That sounded like a terrible idea.

"The species as a whole collects and consumes bones, and they aren't too particular about whether the thing with the bones is dead or not. Ones they think are too pretty get collected while the others..."

At the look on my face, Aemon paused, and his gaze softened. "We don't have to go, you know."

I tried to wrap my head around it. When you thought about it, they weren't much different than ghouls or vampires. Their diet was questionable, but different people ate different shit. I'd just have to remember to not get on its bad side.

Sure.

No problem.

"You wanted to meet with him for a reason. You dragged me all the way to Paris to do it. I'm not leaving this city without talking to the guy, I don't care what he eats for breakfast."

Nope, I totally cared what he ate for breakfast, and

the more I thought about it, the more it gave me the willies. But I hadn't suffered through takeoff and landing in my first flight since high school to not get answers. That was totally not my style. And while the thought of what he might look and *smell* like totally turned my stomach, I was going to get some information, dammit.

"As you wish, Flower. Don't say I didn't warn you."

But he hadn't warned me. He'd given vague hints of a creepy guy, without providing the actual details.

"Bullshit. You wanted to meet him. *Why*?"

Yes, the cop came out of my voice—something I knew he wasn't a fan of, but I just couldn't make myself give a shit. I was inquisitive and untrusting by nature, and that had been *before* Bishop ruined my view on relationships forever.

"I would have told you before but we... *got distracted*." He pinched the bridge of his nose, halting his steps as the city passed us by. "Edoril is supposed to guard a crossroads. A place that could be hidden from Fate and Death. If a certain asshole is hiding there, then..." Aemon trailed off, and my mind started to spin.

I had so many questions.

A crossroads of what? Is that why Bishop was just rolling around undetected? Did he know how to avoid Sloane's gaze? And Fate's?

Was that how Essex had done it for so long?

Aemon restarted his march to the catacombs, taking my hand in his as he led the way down the stairs, the walls surrounding us seeming like a physical chokehold. I could hardly breathe. His fingers tangled with mine were the only thing keeping me from running screaming from the joint as I focused on his answer.

"It's one of many, and based off of who he'd betrayed over the years, I seriously doubt La Roux would be stupid enough to hide in this one. Plus, Edoril would be a good ally to have in all this..." Aemon trailed off as the entrance came into view, putting himself in between the large maw of an opening and me.

And I would have appreciated him being all cute and protective if it didn't make me feel about five years old. We'd have to talk about that shit at some point, but it didn't have to be now.

Even though I really didn't want to, I let his hand go and moved beside him, trying my best to stand tall and *not* reveal my instant fatigue and mounting fear. The call of the souls inside the catacombs was a punch to the gut even from here.

Goodie.

The last thing I wanted was another tunnel incident, but if Edoril had the info I needed, then I was actually going to tough it out this time.

Probably.

I could have a panic attack, too. That was always on the table. In fact, it was even more on the table when the sound of footsteps echoed inside the tunnel. Ghosts—unless they were talking my ear off—did not make much noise.

Bone Fae did.

A thing of nightmares emerged from the opening, and I knew I'd be dreaming about this guy until the end of time and not in a good way. If his gray skin, skull-like facial features, haunting gold eyes, and clothes made of bones and sinew weren't bad enough, it was the blackened talons, bone spear, and the wings that would have done it a thousand times over. I'd always thought bat wings were the scariest, but giant fairy wings with finger-link veining really did put them to shame.

I one thousand percent did not want to go anywhere near this guy, and I had to. *But I really didn't wanna...*

Swallowing hard, I thanked every deity known to man for my poker face. If there was one thing I'd learned in all my years talking to ghosts, it was how to keep a blank expression.

"Edoril," Aemon greeted, his smile gone, his face stoic.

No "How do you do," no "Nice to see ya." Aemon was all business and already ten thousand percent over this shit.

The Fae gave the Prince of Hell a cursory glance, preferring to stare at me with an abandon better suited to a scientist or collector. Did this guy want to keep me, eat me, or fuck me?

Any way he sliced it, it was going to be a hard pass.

"Aemon," he said in heavily accented English—likely for my benefit. "It has been ages. You seemed to have fallen off the map. I worried you had died, old friend."

Either this guy was way more out of the loop than anticipated, or he had an urge to needle Aemon for some reason. Either way, it did not spell good things.

Aemon pasted a false smile on his face. "Just taking a well-needed nap. I was under the impression you wished to share information. Is that not the case?"

Edoril's head tilted to the side in a way that reminded me of a snake—part-jerking, part fluid grace, all inhuman. "Are you not going to introduce me to your friend? How rude you've become in your old age."

The Fae had to be thousands of years old to know Aemon, and his comment implied Aemon was considerably older. *Jesus fuck, how old is he?*

He stepped closer, his spear clacking against the ground with each footfall. Within three feet, he held out his hand—talons, papery gray skin, and all—for me to shake. The southerner in me wanted to take it, but the cop, woman, and grave talker in me?

Solid no.

I stared at the hand without taking it. "I'm not much of a handshake kind of girl. You wanted to see me?"

I wasn't trying to be rude exactly, but I was still butt-hurt about damn near getting swarmed the last time I'd come to visit. And if what Aemon said was true, Edoril knew damn well who and what I was before I'd gotten here the first time and had an inkling of what it would do to me. Unless the Fae wanted an exploded grave talker —*or an all-powerful one*—his first impression wasn't exactly positive.

The Fae withdrew his hand. "Claude tells me you were kind to him. Not many grave talkers are to the long dead, choosing to consume them instead. Tell me—are you any relation to Hildenbrand O'Shea?"

I gave the Fae a winsome smile. "That depends on whether you like him or not. And of course I was kind to Claude. I don't shoot messengers unless they piss me off, and he was perfectly polite. Now, your envoy said you wanted to speak with me. I suggest you get on with whatever it was you had to say."

Edoril's eyes narrowed a little before a chilling smile spread across his skull-like face. "My home drains you, does it not? But only because you choose not to drain the souls from it. You have too much of Azrael in you, child, to not feel the call of the Underworld. I wonder if Faerie calls to you, too."

Did that mean that the crossroads Aemon had spoken of was the Underworld, Faerie, and Earth? No wonder Sloane couldn't see Bishop—if this was where he was hiding. A place like this was likely fucking with her sight in a big way.

Aemon stepped up, his hand on my arm lending me a little of his power without it being too obvious. "Is there a point you wish to make?"

But even if I had gotten a few tidbits of info, this felt too much like a stall. Edoril didn't have anything. If he did, he wouldn't be beating around the bush like this.

Sighing, I reached the end of my patience. "Come on, Aemon. It's time to leave. If he had anything vital to tell us, he wouldn't piss off a grave talker ten feet from an infinite source of power."

Edoril leaned forward, his smile wider this time. "Or I chose to summon you to a place where you would be close to said power on purpose." His gaze left mine and trailed up over my shoulder. "So when enemies came to call, you'd have it on hand."

Trap. Trap, trap, trap. Fuck. I knew I should have brought weapons. Hildy always told me to listen to my gut.

"If I were you, I would duck."

An arm around my middle dragged me out of the way as a red ball of magic exploded the cobblestones where I once stood. I'd recognize that scarlet magic anywhere, and I had a hunch I'd discover a blonde head and child-sized, red-robed form somewhere around here.

The Knoxville ABI were supposed to be looking for Nero's children. Looked like they missed one.

Or maybe more than one.

Blood-red magic rained down from above, pelting the ground like bombs from maybe a hundred of Nero's children. And that lasted all of three seconds before Aemon let out a malevolent growl, his body dissolving into the black smoke of his hellish form.

Darkness filled the alcove, the only spot of light appearing from Aemon's hellfire eyes, his horns, his flaming axe, and the scarlet magic of Nero's children. It hit the dense smoke over and over as Aemon shielded me. And I wanted to help—I did—but the souls were draining my body far faster than I thought they would—even from here.

Without Aemon holding me, I wilted to my knees. Was this how I was going to go out? On my knees while Nero's children finished the job their master had started?

"Draw from the well, child," Edoril whispered, his voice burrowing inside my brain like a drill, even though he was twenty feet away, backing under the shelter of the catacombs. "Help him. Nero's children have been preparing for such a day as they would meet the Prince of Hell again. If you think they don't know how to kill your *âme soeur* you would be sorely mistaken."

Aemon's fiery axe swung, knocking into small, red-robed forms, but for all I knew, it could be that bullshit automaton magic Lars had. The little fucker had made copies of himself that could hit just as hard as he could, but unless you got the fucker at the source, did the copies die.

Edoril wasn't lying. They would kill Aemon if I didn't step up and fucking do something. And when had I ever just sat there and let someone fucking save me?

Never. The answer was never in a million years.

Get your shit together, Darby. Aemon needs you.

I was waffling until I heard Aemon's pained grunt. Until he staggered back, holding his side. Until his dense smoke form was broken up just slightly by a great maw of bloody flesh.

Oh, hell *no.*

The heat of blistering rage lit me up as the scent of ocean water filled my nose. They had burned him with salt. They had corralled us and attacked us and burned him, all because I wouldn't let their fucker of a master kill me.

All because I chose to live.

In an instant, I called souls to me, yanking them from the catacombs akin to ripping off a bandage. Memories and lives filled my brain, but I didn't see any of it. All I noticed was Aemon's demonic form melting away, him staggering to his knees beside me. The fire started bleeding from his eyes as he was still trying to cover me when a salt bomb hit him square in the chest.

He fell to his back, his blistered and burned flesh weeping and exposed. His breaths labored. A thread of fear flashed across his face for the first time maybe ever.

An unholy scream ripped from my lips as I let those souls fill me, the chaos magic igniting in my veins, the death and grave talker and chaos all solidified, gelling together as I let it out. An explosion of golden light detonated in the alcove, rocking the earth as blackness and golden light and fire tore through one red-robed vampire after the other.

The chaos pulled them to me—automaton and master alike—as I burned them from the inside out. Screams echoed off the stone walls, vibrating down the tunnel, as the Underworld called to them. The automatons melted away until a single, red-robed vampire was left, his screams music to my fucking ears.

And I wouldn't be waiting for an interrogation, either. I'd learned that lesson with Astrid.

No, I'd kill first and rifle through his soul for answers after.

Right after I made sure Aemon kept breathing.

Because I would be damned if he was dying on me. Not this man, and not on my fucking watch.

He wasn't dying.

I'd make sure of it.

8

Watching a vampire burn to death was not high on my bucket list.

There was that whole screaming thing and the wailing and the pleading for death that just turned my stomach. To avoid the annoyance, I let the chaos free, slicing his head off with a blade of golden light.

I'd think about how I learned that particular skill later, and why it irritated the fuck out of me that I actually got something of benefit from being with Bishop.

But I didn't even have the luxury of enjoying the vampire's head plopping to the ground.

I was too busy making sure Aemon didn't follow Nero's child into the fucking afterlife and taking my stupid, cursed heart with him. As beat up as he was, I had no idea where I could even touch him without causing him more pain. Was this what he felt like when I'd been dying? This utter helplessness that made me want to follow him if he went.

My nose and eyes burned with tears I refused to shed as the threat of losing him loomed over our heads. I'd never seen him even a little weak, and for him to be brought low made panic bloom in my gut as fury ignited in my blood.

Aemon's breath sawed through his lungs, his blue eyes wide with fear and pain and... uncertainty. We'd been caught off guard, walked right into a trap, and if I didn't figure this out, I was going to lose him.

I really didn't want to lose him.

"It's okay. You're okay," I soothed, as bile rose in my throat. He was in so much pain and he was trying to hide it and it made me want to kill that fucking vampire twice. "I'm going to help you."

I'd thought he'd been joking on the plane about the saltwater burning him to death. I'd almost laughed at his quip. Now I knew it for the truth it was. Aemon's soul burned bright, yes, but it was fading too fast, and I swore if I saw my sister anywhere near him...

His shaking hand latched onto my wrist, his weeping skin almost cracking as he gripped me so tight. "N-no, Fflower. I'll h-heal on my own." He let out a mirthless breath that was far too pained to be anything close to the chuckle he wanted it to be. "I've seen how you give of y-yourself."

That wasn't fair.

Sure, sometimes I was a Class-A martyr with a death wish, and the particular time he was speaking of, it was Jay who had been dying in my arms. He was my best friend. Of course I would pick him over me. At the time, I didn't have much in the way of things to live *for*.

And Jay did. He had a family and a cute boyfriend and a job and a *life*. At the time all I had was a boatload of dead parents, a wonky job, and an epic boyfriend betrayal. I hadn't exactly been bowling strikes.

But that was then, and this was now.

I didn't want to die in Aemon's stead. I wanted him to live. *With me.*

And no, I was not thinking about what that meant, either. I wasn't thinking about what would happen if I couldn't help him or why I needed him to be okay. That would be for later when he wasn't actively dying on me, and my heart didn't feel like it was being carved out of my chest with a rusty scalpel.

"The fuck you will. I wasn't asking, Aemon." I was juiced up with enough to spare. The power from the souls was practically leaking from my skin, and he wanted to bring up old shit.

Shoving energy into him, I watched as his back bowed off the ground, a howl of agony ripping up his throat as his skin knitted back together. And I felt every bit of it with him. An echo of his pain leeched into me as he healed, the excruciating burns and weeping sores fading to nothing. But that didn't stop my heart from feeling like he was a hairsbreadth from leaving me forever. Aemon's breath eased, the pinch of fear and pain in his brow smoothed.

But me?

It was as if he were still dying. I knew he was all better, but I had to give him more. He needed protection. He needed to never get burned like that again. Aemon needed to be safe. He needed to always be safe.

"You have to stop, Flower."

With enough chaos magic and the souls still left in that tunnel, I could protect him—make it so Nero's children or Bishop or anyone else couldn't do this to him. Shaking my head, I shoved more power into him. I wanted his skin damn near impenetrable.

"Darby, Flower, you have to stop." He sat up, cupping my cheeks in his hands. "I'm all better. You're not going to lose me. I wasn't dying, I swear."

But he was. He was *dying* trying to protect me.

I latched onto his wrists, that tightness not leaving me for a second. Nose burning, eyes tearing, my whole body shook as I struggled to take in a full breath.

"Yes, you were."

Aemon pressed his lips to my forehead, pulling me into his chest. He wrapped his arms around me, but still, the panic was there. It burrowed down and made a home in my chest. There was no getting rid of it.

Not now.

"Oh, how sweet you two are," Edoril crooned, and for a split second, I didn't feel fear at all.

No, that same rage when Aemon staggered to the ground engulfed my gut in the hottest of blazes. I wrenched out of Aemon's hold and launched myself at the Fae, two blades of golden light bracketing his neck as he laid plastered to the ground before either of us had time to blink.

"If I were you, I'd start talking. *Now*."

Edoril's skull-like face blanked of all expression. "You think I did this?"

"I think you called us here when we were perfectly happy not ever coming back. I think no one tried to melt his skin off until you made us come talk to you. I think if I wanted to point fingers at someone for being shady, it most certainly would be you." I leaned forward, letting the magic in my hand drift oh, so close to his face. "I think you'd better state your case. I've already cut one person's head off tonight. Care to make it two?"

"You are nothing like your father. You and that sister of yours are more vicious than Azrael by leaps and bounds. But out of the two, you're the hothead. I wonder if that's why Azrael made sure your sister took his wings and not you."

I fought off the urge to laugh. Sloane was far more vicious, and her body count was still higher than mine. And I had never wanted Azrael's job. I'd rather be the one solving the murders instead of sending souls to their rest.

"Cute. Trying to do the whole 'sisterly rivalry' thing, but I never wanted the wings, Edoril, and stalling will not let you keep your head. I want to know why you sold us out, and if there are any more of Nero's children waiting for us on the other side of that wall. Talk, or I will glean it from your fucking bones."

Two years ago, I would have never interrogated a suspect this way. Now, it seemed like it would just be easier to kill first. At the very least it would be faster.

"He paid me in the bones of his sisters and brothers, asking to use my contact with Aemon to lure him here."

I hissed at the gut punch of his betrayal, fighting off the urge to just lop off his head and be done with it. Sure, Fae were usually tricky bastards—Jimmy excluded—but damn. I'd never crossed this guy, never said a bad word to him, and he wanted to just serve us up? For bones?

Bones?

"Why?" I seethed through gritted teeth.

Edoril rolled his eyes like I was a special brand of stupid. "Based off how you two acted in my home, I knew you would be together, and I knew you had the ability to kill the vampire should the desire strike. I also neglected to advise the vampire of just how many souls were lurking in my home. He assumed he had the upper hand. He did not."

But that little bit of maneuvering didn't mean a damn thing to me. "You gambled with our lives over a pile of bones and ash?"

I'd not taken kindly to Bishop gambling with my life when he was my fucking boyfriend, and I sure as shit didn't like it any more then.

"What would you rather I deal in? Money? Bits of paper and coin that mean nothing until someone gives them value? Why would I deal in something so trivial? Bones have power, a magic so potent, it allows me to guard a place such as this. Allows me to put a foot in not just one, but three worlds."

If he was guarding a crossroads, he was doing a shit job of it.

"I care about the 'selling us out' bit a fuck of a lot

more than your method of payment," Aemon rumbled at my side, his heat and warmth and life only slightly the balm I needed it to be.

"It was less a sellout and more a double-cross. I owe you too much to—"

Aemon's growl rattled my bones as his axe formed in his hand. "Put me in direct line of fire of salt bombs? Getting my skin damn near melted off? Getting my woman frightfully close to being murdered? You thought you owed me before? You owe me a *fuck* of a lot more now."

If he could conjure his magic, maybe he really would be okay—even if said magic hadn't quite helped him here.

"She should take your head and have her sister dump your double-crossing ass into the pit. Maybe I'll let my brothers have you. See what they think of salt bombs and double-crosses. You know, I was going to ask her to back off, but now that I think about it, why should she? Why should she show you a crumb of leniency?"

Edoril's face split wide, his smile fucking frightening to say the least. It was a knowing smile, a teasing one. Like he knew something we didn't and was just waiting for one of us to ask the question.

"Because I know where Bishop La Roux was yesterday."

I swear to everything holy, if he's lying to me, I'll destroy everything he loves while he watches and then burn him to ash.

But a part of me cared less about Bishop and far more that he put Aemon in harm's way. And that part was getting louder and louder the more Edoril's silence stretched on.

"I hope you're not waiting on an engraved invitation, Sugar. I'm starting to quit caring what you know and far more interested in what your blood will look like on the outside of your body."

Edoril's smile grew wider, like I was a yipping puppy nipping at his heels. Nodding, I moved a single blade, embedding it in his gut and slicing up. Black blood oozed from the wound as shock hit the Fae's face for the first time since I dropped him.

"I would like answers," I said, so calmly it was in direct opposition to the glowing, magic-spun knife in his belly. "Now."

Edoril's mouth gaped open and closed like a fish out of water. "L-la Roux knew France was off-limits to him b-but he came here anyway. No one w-would deal w-with a La Roux mage. N-not a-after his father n-nearly de-destroyed all the Fae in France. B-but he s-still wanted to d-deal. Y-you just m-missed him. By maybe an hour. H-he's using the crossroads. Hiding in plain sight."

"What did he promise you?" Aemon asked, his question a good one.

Guaranteed, if Bishop promised him anything, it was likely a lie. He was good at that.

"Death," Edoril whispered, his smile wider than it had ever been. "Freedom. Rest. He promised if I needled her enough, she would send me to the afterlife. Looks like he was right."

And damn if I wasn't going to make that lousy, no-good motherfucker a liar.

Smiling, I poured magic into Edoril as I ripped the blade from his gut, healing his wounds up all nice and tight. Yes, I took more souls to do it, but it was a fair price to pay to spite Bishop.

Spite was a hell of a motivator, after all.

Fuck him and his Fae deal.

"Wrong. You keep making deals with that bastard, and I'll make sure Death never comes for you. I'll make sure she lets you rot on this plane forever. And when this place finally crumbles and there is nothing left, there won't be an ounce of rest or freedom. Only pain and toil."

I yanked him to his feet, lifting the giant of a Fae over my head by his bone necklace. "And unlike Bishop La Roux, I keep my promises."

9

I was going to be sick.

After Edoril scurried back inside his little hidey-hole, I decided absorbing Nero's child would be a fabulous idea. *Spoiler alert: it was not a good idea.* It was probably the worst idea I'd ever had, and I'd had some whoppers in my past.

But I needed the info Edoril was hesitant to give me —*still*—and I needed it from a reliable source. Since I trusted the Bone Fae about as much as I did Bishop, absorbing the little shit was my only option. But as soon as his soul touched me, I knew it had been the worst idea maybe ever.

Oskar was six when he'd been turned. *Six.* That alone was enough to make me barf, but it actually managed to get worse. He'd loved Nero like a father and was one of his most loyal foot soldiers. He was also a bona fide serial killer, psychopath, and sadist. His favorite pastime was stripping the skin off of human women and feeding it to his snakes before drinking them down.

No numbing. No trancing. Just screams, pain, and death.

His body count was in the tens of thousands, and he for damn sure knew what he was doing. From what I gathered, this was a common problem in children turned before puberty—aside from the totally gross and downright evil practice that Nero was famous for. Children very rarely were able to avoid killing their victims. No matter their age, no matter their control, being around that much death for long enough made anyone a monster.

Out of all of Nero's children, he was one of the few who made it out of Knoxville. The little shit had followed us all the way across the Atlantic with the singular focus of making sure neither Aemon nor I made it out of here. He'd also hated Bishop probably more than I did, and after he killed us, my ex was next on his to-do list. Solid proof that a broken clock was right twice a day.

The only useful thing I'd gleaned from his demented little soul? Bishop was indeed using the crossroads to hide. Unfortunately, someone like Oskar couldn't follow him. The pull of the Underworld was too strong for an ancient dead thing. Only the living could traverse so close to a gate without going in. He'd been waiting for Bishop to get far enough away from the entrance and then it would have been over.

Other than a life full of awful, deplorable sadism and murder, Oskar didn't have much in the way of information, and that pissed me off. I should have left his ghost to roam the earth, unable to hurt anyone. Then again, if there was a specter able to figure out just how fast they could turn poltergeist, it would be one of Nero's children.

No, thank you.

The absolute last thing I needed was a berserker of a child vampire causing more havoc in this world. Still, vomiting was on the table, and I was for sure going to need mind bleach for this soul. Shuddering, I tried not to gag and tried to think happy thoughts.

It totally wasn't working.

"Vodka, water, or coffee?" Aemon asked, helping me walk away from Edoril's home and back to the fresh air of Paris. I gulped it in. Sure, the "fresh" part of the air was suspect just like with any big city, but it was air not anywhere close to a catacomb, so I'd take it.

After what I just saw?

"Vodka. No... *tequila*. I could use a few brain cells to

die off. Maybe it'll make me forget what just defiled my brain."

Honestly, I'd prefer an amnesiac, but those were harder to come by. I would really enjoy permanently erasing the last hour from my memory bank.

"As you wish."

Aemon closed his arms around me, and the faint pull of his whisking me off to wherever dipped my stomach a bit. But when our feet touched down, I had to fight off a gasp.

We'd landed in our bedroom in the villa, sure, but the room was not how we'd left it. The bed was in ruins, the mattress slashed to ribbons while the bedframe sat lopsided and broken in half. The mirrors were in pieces on the floor and the chandelier was flickering and hanging by one sparking wire from the ceiling. My clothes were cut to ribbons, my toiletries strewn everywhere.

"Please tell me we did not destroy this place with our marathon sex. I didn't miss all this, right?" I mean, that sex was a solid twenty out of ten, so it was possible, but *damn.*

Aemon corralled me behind him, his body dissolving into dense smoke as his flaming axe formed in his hand from nothing.

"No, Flower, we did not do this."

If we hadn't done this, I had an inkling I knew who did, and the thought of him going through our things, of being in this room, made me ill. I took Aemon's lead, using the chaos or death magic or just plain old grave talker weirdness and formed the golden light blade in my hand. Luckily, it was at will this time, but I was really wishing I had a gun in my hand, too. Had I known we were flying private, I would have fixed that particular glitch.

Following him, we cleared the bedroom and every other, finding no one. What we did find was a shit-ton of damage and a note in blood on the wall of the dining room. Whose blood, I didn't know, but by the smell, it wasn't an animal's.

Thanks for Oskar. I'll remember that favor when I rip the chaos from your bones. –B

Edoril had said we'd missed him by an hour. When he'd said it, I'd thought we'd missed Bishop by an hour the first time we'd come to visit. That bastard of a Fae had stalled us.

"I should have killed that fucking Fae when I had the chance," Aemon growled, echoing my thoughts exactly. "As much as he owes me and still the fucker does this? I have a feeling Bael and Zephyr would love to hear about his little betrayal."

But I had other concerns.

"Whose blood is that?" I whispered, wondering if we were going to find a dead body around here somewhere. Or worse, have it be Bishop's own blood to fuel a spell of some kind.

"On that note, I believe it's time to leave, Flower. *Now.*"

Aemon must have thought the same damn shit I did because the both of us backed away from the macabre note like it was a fucking bomb. Half a second later, Aemon had his arms around me, and we were outside on the lawn, about a football field away.

Two seconds after that?

An explosion rocked the earth and Aemon and I hit the dirt, him covering me with his body. By the time I looked back, the villa was on fire.

And not just a little fire, either. No, it was a five-alarm style, "burn everything to ashes" kind of fire.

This wasn't the first time I'd nearly lost everything— including my life—to a blaze, but damn if it didn't sting. It made me glad I hadn't brought my father's note with me on this trip. That was sitting in a safety deposit box in Knoxville under enough wards to keep the paper from so much as crinkling until the end of time.

Maybe I'd read it one day, but until then, it'd be safe nowhere near me.

"Are you all right, Flower?"

Maybe Aemon asked because he worried I was hurt. Or maybe it was because I was covering my mouth with my hand as I stared at the beautiful sprawling home be reduced to rubble.

Did rentals have ex-boyfriend insurance?

"He destroyed a piece of history to be a dick. He nearly killed us. He... How are we going to pay for this? Wha—"

My tirade was cut off by Aemon's lips on mine. "I meant, are you hurt? I could give a fuck about the house. I can rebuild it if I choose. I care about you."

Oh. Oh, no. Not only had Bishop defiled the bed where Aemon and I had come together, he'd...

"That wasn't a rental, was it?"

Aemon's smile stretched across his mouth as he shook his head. "No."

"That was your house, wasn't it?"

Aemon nodded and I felt sick again. Bishop hadn't destroyed a rental that no one lived in. This was Aemon's home. Aemon had taken me to his home.

Tears hit my eyes as I returned my gaze to the flames. Pieces of the roof were starting to cave in. I had looked the place over with a cursory glance of a rental. Had I known it was actually his, I would have paid more attention.

"It's one of many," he said offhandedly. "They can be replaced."

But he didn't get it. He didn't get just how important it was to me.

"You brought me to your home."

He tilted his head like I was confusing him. "Of course I did. But that isn't my home. It's where I lay my head when I'm in this country. It's a house. Just a house."

He opened his mouth to say something else but snapped it shut as he curled me into his arms. "We should talk to Sloane. She needs to know how Bishop is avoiding her sight. I have a feeling the Fates would like to know as well."

That was a good idea, sure. But I had no idea how I could ever repay what Bishop had taken away from him.

Bishop could have killed him—killed us. He could have made the place explode with salt bombs or... Aemon needed more protection. He needed to be safe. Breath tried and failed to saw through my lungs. Bishop wanted to take everything away from me. He'd nearly taken Jay, nearly taken my life. And now—

"You should go back to Hell. You'll be safe there. No way would he follow you." I pushed away from him, lifting a shaking hand to my mouth as I stared at what had become of Aemon's home. "You should get away from me."

Save yourself. Please just keep yourself safe.

It was one thing to be having fun with each other as we did this, but if Aemon stayed with me, he was going to get hurt. Hadn't he already? He'd damn near died in my arms less than an hour ago. Finding Bishop was too dangerous. I was probably too stupid to be doing this by myself, too, but if it meant that—

"Please tell me I didn't hear what I thought I just did. Please tell me you aren't using this as an excuse to send me away."

Blinking, I returned my gaze to Aemon, registering for the first time that he was pissed off. *Really* pissed off. Fire eyes, horns, and all.

"I—"

"If the words coming out of your mouth aren't that you were taking the piss, then I don't want to fucking hear it." He loomed over me, stalking with an animal's grace as he backed me up step by step. "Because if you recall, I told you I wasn't letting you go. I don't lie, Darby. Not ever. You said you understood, but I don't think you do. I'm *not* letting you go. Not. Ever. Not when it's hard. Not when you're being the most stubborn woman on the planet. Not when you push me away, and not when your bastard of an ex burns down one of my houses."

My back hit a tree, and I couldn't back up anymore.

"Do you understand now? I'm not leaving you. I'm

not going to be anywhere but at your side. I'm not meant to be anywhere else but here. You're mine. I don't leave what's mine." He bracketed his arms on either side of me, pinning me in. "Have I made myself perfectly clear?"

Okay, so maybe this isn't just a fling for him.

Maybe he was telling the truth when he said all those things.

Maybe...

"I think I might be getting it now." But did I trust it? Did I trust anything?

Aemon leaned down, his fire eyes seeming to blaze right through me as he lifted me right off my feet, pressing my back against the tree before nipping at my bottom lip. His heat filtered through me, stealing that cold pit of dread as soon as I saw that note.

"You let me know if I need to give you a reminder."

He blinked, the fire fading to the crystalline blue that burned me in a whole different way. "Or maybe I should fuck you so hard you never stop feeling me. Maybe you should carry my mark. That way you never forget."

Mark? What did he mean by that? Did I care? All I wanted was his lips on mine. I wanted a reminder that he was alive—that we were alive.

"I need you," I whispered against his lips before he took my mouth in a searing kiss.

It was a start, but the scream of sirens in the distance told me I wasn't going to get everything I wanted.

Aemon set me down but didn't let me go. "Now, let's get out of here, yes?"

Shakily, I nodded. We did need to leave, and when we did, it needed to be to a place Bishop wouldn't think to go —somewhere he wasn't welcome or couldn't enter.

"Where?"

Aemon's smile was practically sinful.

"I know a place."

10

Aemon's "place" had a very odd feeling to it.

Similar to the vibration in my bones in the tunnel, it was just *off* in a way I couldn't put my finger on. That wasn't to say that the home at the end of the lane wasn't completely gorgeous—it was—but I had a feeling we weren't in Kansas anymore.

Maybe it was the turrets or the sheer size of the place or the gardens leading up to the largest fucking house I'd ever seen, but I felt like I stuck out like a sore thumb. Would I have to curtsey at some point? Because it didn't matter that I had taken all the etiquette courses possible, I was *not* a lady.

"Come on, Flower," Aemon urged, pulling me behind him at a quick clip. "I want to show you my home."

Had anyone melted the ice around my heart with a single sentence before? This was Aemon's *home*. Not a house, not a property. *His home.* My reluctant feet picked up speed.

The grounds were beautiful. Ancient trees reached for the heavens as thick moss cushioned our steps. Clusters of wildflowers dotted the field and bees buzzed lazily from one to another. There didn't seem to be a rush, no urgency that weighed down every step and every heartbeat.

"Where are we?" It had to be another country, if not a whole other continent. And how had we gotten here if he couldn't go over an ocean? How was it daytime?

Aemon just smiled as the gates opened to admit us. "Promise you won't freak out?"

That did nothing for the flock of bats masquerading as butterflies in my stomach, stealing the peace that had just taken root.

"No." He knew better than to ask me that. When had I ever *not* freaked out?

Never. The answer was never.

He stopped us, hooking an arm around me and pulling me close. Aemon was the only one who could do that and not have it feel pretentious. And no, I was not thinking about why he could do that and no one else could, either. Even spelling me to the moon and back hadn't given Bishop the ability to pull that off.

You know what this means.

Nope. Means nothing. Not a damn thing.

It does. You know it does.

"Even if I promise you're safe and nothing will harm you here?"

That knocked all the lovey-dovey shit out of my brain.

He didn't. Someone, somewhere, please tell me this fool didn't bring me to the one place where I most definitely should not be.

"We're in the Underworld?" I screeched, scaring the shit out of some birds as they escaped a nearby tree. "When I said I wanted a place where Bishop couldn't follow, I didn't think I had to be dead to get it, Aemon. What the fuck?"

I was gearing up for the mother of all freak-outs when Aemon cupped my jaw and dropped a kiss so *scorching* to my lips, I thought I was going to combust on the spot.

How the fuck does he do that?

"You're not dead, Flower. You're just visiting. You're a demigod for Fate's sake—a Daughter of Death. Why would you not be able to come and go from the Underworld as you pleased?"

I squinted at him, my brain half-scrambled from that kiss. "I distinctly remember Sloane having to cough up toes to get here a little bit ago. I sacrificed no toes. Hence the confusion. Explain."

Aemon's expression was three steps past horrified. "Who in the bloody hell made her sacrifice toes?" Then he did a full-body shudder like the thought revolted him.

Join the club, buddy.

"Wait," he said, seeming to think on it. "Did she come on her own?"

That had my steps stuttering. "No. Bastian, Thomas, and Axel went with her, but the spell didn't work on Thomas, so he had to turn around and come back."

Aemon nodded, resuming his walk and dragging me behind him. "That's it then. The toes weren't for her entry, they were so she could bring guests. You aren't with someone who shouldn't be here, so payment for passage is irrelevant. I was born in the Underworld."

It took me a while to process that little tidbit—long enough that I was dumbstruck by the doors seeming to open by themselves and the opulence of the home itself. It was part castle, part Victorian manor, and all class. It actually seemed like an amalgamation of all my dream houses on my Pinterest board mixed with shit I had no idea even existed.

The entry staircase was the real wonder. It looked like

it was part tree branches, part iron work, and part intricate woodwork mixed together to form the most beautiful thing I'd ever seen. And the books. It was as if the Beast's library had gotten its blueprints from this house. Every place my eyes touched had the same quality —unearthly beauty that felt so familiar and not, all at the same time.

And under all the beauty and the pretty architecture and the bit of joy I was feeling at having him show me his space, my heart ached something awful.

I was in the Underworld. There had been so many times I'd wanted to come here but never asked. So many times I wanted to ask but couldn't. Because if she'd have told me no, I would have resented her forever.

My dad was somewhere around here, and I didn't know if I was allowed to see him or not.

"We'll need to talk to Sloane and the Fates, but I need to grab payment first. Do you want a tour, or—"

"I want to see my father," I blurted, a fleeting bit of hope burrowing inside me. "Killian Adler, I mean. I know Azrael is gone forever, but..." I trailed off, unable to even look at him.

I want my dad.

If his face had pity on it or censure, it would end me. I was starting to ignore all the bias and warnings in my brain and listen to my heart for once. All it would take was one look on his face to ruin it.

And ruining it would be the absolute worst thing.

Because you're fall—

No. Nope. Stop that shit right now.

Aemon's hand found mine and he dropped a kiss to my temple. "I'll grab more coins, then. The ferryman will want his payment."

Only then did I look up into his crystalline blue gaze. "We'll head there first, yes?"

Tears welled in my eyes as a watery chuckle broke free of my chest. "Okay."

"I bet you're not mad we're in the Underworld now, are you?"

Rising on my toes, I pressed a kiss to those dangerously sexy lips. "I'm not mad."

And I wasn't. Time was on pause in the Underworld. When Sloane went, she'd been gone for days, and it had only been a few minutes for us. That meant we weren't in a rush here. I could breathe—we could breathe. I could rest. I could...

"I need you, Aemon," I whispered against his lips.

In answer, he lifted me off my feet, carrying me up the stairs as he seared my mouth in a kiss so blistering it had me tearing off his clothes, as the ache in my middle damn near drove me insane.

I didn't have responsibilities or worries.

I didn't have a job or a mission.

For this brief moment in time, all I had was Aemon, this kiss, and hopefully a bed.

"I'm cashing in on that offer for you to fuck me so hard I never stop feeling you." But that was only because I had no idea what a mark from a demon prince meant. I had a feeling it was why he wouldn't bite me in bed, and for some reason, it made me want it more. It made me want all of him.

But more than that, I wanted to have this little piece of happiness.

I wanted it so fucking bad I could taste it.

And I wanted it with him.

"As you wish, Flower," he murmured against my lips, stalking through the halls until he found the room he was looking for. "As you wish."

The first time Aemon had ever said those words to me, it had been me sending him away. He'd helped me sleep after days of insomnia from fear and anxiety. But he'd been too perceptive, knowing before I had that there were people in my life that shouldn't be there. I'd bitten his head off, ordering him to leave me alone.

Now the thought of sending him away made my heart clench in my chest.

I wanted him closer—needed him closer.

A moment later, I found my back on a bed and Aemon pulling off my boots.

He could have snapped his fingers to undress me, but he took his time, peeling each garment off like he was unwrapping a present. His gaze worshipped me, lovingly caressing every part of my exposed skin, and it was as if it were a physical touch.

By the time I was naked, my patience had shattered.

A snap of my fingers later, and he was just as naked as I was, the chaos yanking him to me like we were magnets. His mouth crashed into mine as his fingers twined in my hair.

"Tell me what your mark means," I ordered against his mouth, needing this bit of information, and not knowing why. "Is it like a shifter thing?"

Aemon's gaze blazed with the fire of his demon. "No," he growled, notching himself against my sex. "A shifter's mate is picked by Fate. A demon chooses who they love, who they wish to spend forever with. I've never bitten a lover—never even wanted to. Not until you."

My breath caught in my chest as his words and cock filled me at the same time.

"It's not time, Flower. You aren't ready for forever. Just know it's on the table, yes?"

I wasn't ready for forever, but he was. All he was waiting on was me to tell him I was with him.

"But until then, I'm going to fuck you like you're mine."

Slowly, I nodded, and Aemon got busy showing me exactly what being his meant.

And I loved every second.

11

Curled up with Aemon in his bed, I slept better than I had in months—years, even. In fact, I didn't realize how tired I was until I woke up refreshed, plastered to his chest, and his rumbling breaths underneath me.

Aemon sleeping was something else, too: his brow smooth and his dark-blond lashes fanning out over the top of his cheeks and the way he clutched me to him even in rest.

Yep, I was a goner. There was little denying it now.

Typically, I was a "cuddle and roll" kind of girl, but with Aemon, I had the urge to just melt into him like he was my own personal pillow. He was a drug, a balm. The kind of medicine that healed the parts of you that you had no idea were even broken.

Reaching up, I nipped at his full bottom lip, earning me a slow, sleepy smile as he dragged me up his body before easily flipping me over and blowing a raspberry on my neck. My back pressed into the bed, I laughed at his antics, marveling at the stupid joy of it all. Somehow, we ended up tangled together, his crystalline eyes never breaking from mine as he worshipped me over and over again.

It took ages to peel ourselves out of bed, my squalling stomach doing the job for us. It was funny, while I missed coffee, I didn't need it. That didn't stop Aemon from brewing me a pot while I threw on one of his silk robes, brushed my teeth, and took care of my bladder—proof I wasn't dead if there ever was one.

Padding down the stairs, I got lost twice trying to find Aemon, only managing to follow my nose to the kitchen. Just like everything else in this house—what little I'd seen of it—the kitchen was a mix of opulent luxury and whimsical charm, like he'd plucked exactly what my dream house would be right out of my brain and made it so.

Aemon had a steaming cup of coffee on the counter next to his hip, the picture of shirtless sexy. Clad in nothing but navy pajama bottoms and a smile, it was tough not to ignore the coffee altogether and destroy his kitchen just like we'd done his bed.

Rising on my tiptoes, I gave him a minty kiss in thank you—a kiss that had the potential to make me forget coffee even existed.

Almost.

"Are we interrupting?" my sister asked from behind me, making me freeze completely. Coupling that with a manly chuckle that was not Aemon's, I had a feeling who the "we" was in this scenario. Pulling back, I met Aemon's smiling eyes with my own. "They've been there the whole time, haven't they?"

Aemon nodded. "But I wasn't going to turn down that kiss. Apologies, Flower."

"She lets him call her 'Flower'? You've got big brass ones, mate," Bastian rumbled from his perch next to my sister at the island. A silvery wedding band on his left ring finger gleamed in the sunlight streaming through the window as he lifted a mug to his lips.

"You got married?" I griped, staring at Bastian's ring like it had personally done me wrong. "Without telling anyone?"

My gaze whipped from my sister to her husband and back, the shock doing me in.

Did I have more pressing matters—like how I was naked under this robe and that my sister and her husband now totally knew I was having wild monkey sex with a Prince of Hell?

Yes, I did.

But my sister got married and I didn't know it.

Sloane snorted into her coffee mug, the light catching on the giant purple rock on her finger. Well, didn't that just beat all.

"What the fuck, dude?" Sloane was my only blood relation left on the planet. I would have thought...

Shrugging, she rested her head on Bastian's shoulder. "We didn't do the whole wedding thing. It was pretty much he asked, I said yes, and then I may have conjured a band for him, and that was it. The whole 'wedding thing' isn't my style."

Well, she wasn't wrong there. Sloane's idea of dressing up was cleaning the blood off her combat boots.

"Fine, if you want to be all logical about it. Any other news I missed?"

Sloane waffled her hand. "Unless you count Fate being a pain?"

That was something that didn't make sense to me. "Is she one person or three people? The mythology is confusing as fuck."

Aemon chuckled as he pulled me close. "Depends on the day. Sometimes she is one person—the spinner, measure, and cut all in one. Other days she splits into three—the maid, mother, and crone. People get her confused with Hecate all the time, and Homer wasn't the best at sticking to a plotline."

That explained the confusion. "I think I know why. Does it have to do with our little problem and how he keeps avoiding her sight? Because I think I might know how he's doing it."

I'd go into the assassination attempt and how he planned on stripping the chaos from me later.

Sloane's eyes lit with malice and the smile on her face was three steps past wrathful.

"I'm all ears."

I had no interest in ever meeting Fate, or the Fates, or whatever the fuck they were calling themselves at the moment. After the way she'd done me wrong in the past, I couldn't say we would ever be on good terms. I mean, the dads dying and losing the mom lottery and the boyfriend drama all while being slapped with the grave talker albatross?

Talk about *rude.*

Had I pissed she—*them*—off in a past life? Did she enjoy sticking it to Azrael so much that I was their new plaything? Any way you sliced it, I'd been done dirty— the Aemon events in his bedroom notwithstanding. If anything, what that man could do with his tongue should be considered payback after the bullshit they'd pulled.

And while all that was true, I was still on this lady's doorstep when I should have been in Elysium visiting my dad.

"Explain to me why I need to be here," I griped, searching for an escape.

I was last in line while Sloane knocked on a carved wooden door that fit better in a Grimm fairytale than this corner of the Underworld, but whatever. I could escape and find my own damn way to Elysium.

Probably.

"Because your presence was requested," Sloane said for the tenth time while I tried not to say what I'd said the first time she insisted on me coming.

I had a feeling if I said that particular insult within earshot, I'd regret it.

A woman of indeterminate age whipped the door open, her bubblegum-pink hair in distinct opposition to her leaf-green eyes and solidly goth-style clothes. The all-leather corset and pants combo coupled with the pencil-thin stilettos was a bit of a shock, but I had to admire her style.

Her gaze went straight to mine before she sashayed from the door without so much as a "hello."

Sloane and Bastian followed her inside, but I had the strongest urge to run. I had shit to do, after all. I'd done my due diligence. I'd told Sloane about the blind spot.

Anything after that was going above and beyond. Plus, she was Fate. She could probably glean the story from Sloane.

"Usually, I have to kick people out," a smooth voice called from inside the house, "not beg them to come in."

Grumbling, I allowed Aemon to lead me inside. It was supposed to be sex, food, Elysium. Not sex, food, tromping through the Underworld. She was dicking with my plans.

"You're big on those. *Plans*," Fate said as she peeled an orange with a paring knife, her long legs crossed at the knee as she bounced her foot impatiently.

Sloane sat across from her with Bastian at her back, staring at Fate like she was trying to figure her out. If Sloane couldn't do it, I doubted I could. My little sister had powers of the mind I just didn't have.

Still, this felt like a digging kind of mission.

Too bad when it came to me, there was nothing to find. I wasn't big on secrets, and I didn't want to know the future.

So why am I here?

"Was that supposed to be a question or a statement?" I asked, conjuring myself a seat from thin air. It seemed if no one was going to offer me one, I might as well make one myself. "Because yes, I liked to make plans. I also knew to pivot when necessary. This"—I gestured to the house and her orange peeling—"does not seem necessary."

Fate's gaze went to Sloane. "You were correct. She is a direct one."

Sloane sighed like this was taking centuries off her life. "You knew that already. You know everything already. What's with the"—She waved a hand at the knife —"theatrics?"

Good to know I wasn't the only one annoyed.

Fate stopped peeling her orange and looked me over. "You really don't want to know anything? Your future, your end, whether you get married? Have kids? Where your enemy is right now?"

Kids weren't on the table for someone like me. I had never had the desire to become a mother—never wanted to disappoint a kid like my mother had disappointed me. Sure, when I was little it was because I thought my mother died, but now? I had somehow managed to not get the shitty end of the stick when it came to both of my parents' darker qualities. No way was I going to pass that shit down.

And marriage? That was a solid maybe, but knowing didn't change that. Knowing when I would die? That didn't sit well with me. I didn't want any of what she offered and the shit I did want, she couldn't give me.

"If you could tell me where Bishop was, I wouldn't be

here informing you of a blind spot in your vision. As for the rest? No, thanks. I prefer not knowing."

I was so used to Sarina not being able to tell me anything, that sitting down with the real Fate wasn't much in the way of mind-bending. Sure, she was pretty and a little frightening, but I'd learned firsthand how knowing things made you too confident to how the circumstances could change.

"You really mean that." Fate's eyebrows seemed glued to her hairline. "Did you know since the dawn of time, I have never found anyone who refuses to know their future? Who wants nothing from me. Who only wishes to give me information and no more?"

That… sounded awful. And familiar.

"Even your sister has asked after her friends, her love, her family. But you… other than finding your enemy, you don't want to know anything."

I thought about my father in my arms as he took his last breaths. About Jay pouring blood from his neck. I had no control over those situations and knowing beforehand wouldn't have changed them a bit.

"What would knowing change? Other than making me worry more, I mean? I can't make you give me an easy life, and even if I could, I wouldn't. Because when shit goes sideways, I get to blame you, and that is really satisfying."

I stood, snapping my fingers to get rid of the extra seat. "Now, to why I came. You have a blind spot. The place where Earth, the Underworld, and Faerie meet. If you can't find someone, dollars to doughnuts, that's where they are." I grabbed Aemon's hand and pivoted on a heel, ready to get the hell out of there. "If you'll excuse me—"

"I like you," Fate announced like she was surprised herself. "Azrael's children have been a pain in my ass for eons, but you two... I actually like."

Turning, I pinned her with a raised eyebrow. Silence was always a good interrogation tactic, but it wouldn't work on her. What was "waiting her out" to a woman that had been alive before mankind?

"Thanks?" I muttered, unsure where she was going with this.

Fate stood, waltzing toward me with an enigmatic look in her eyes.

"Stay still," she ordered right before she pressed a soft kiss to my forehead, much like Azrael had before he'd... he'd...

Unlike with Azrael, I didn't feel a giant surge of power or a great healing from something that had been killing me. It wasn't anything other than awkward, really, and I supposed that was just fine. I didn't need another damn person to be giving me any more power. It was bad enough I had to protect Shiloh's chaos from a bitchy ex-boyfriend.

Fate snorted as she drew back. "I do like you, Darby, even though you think I've been cruel to you. I can't say your luck will always be good, but you'll make it work. You always do."

"Thanks?" I offered, marching double-time toward the door.

Fate would likely always give me the willies, but at least she hadn't been mean.

As soon as we made it to the other side of the door, I shot Aemon a "what the fuck" expression. He simply shrugged. Yeah, it hadn't made a damn bit of sense to me, either.

"Come on, Flower. We have a boat to catch."

12

The ferry to Elysium sat on the shores of a black ocean, the sun glittering off the water as it lapped against the dark wooden hull. A hooded figure stood at the bow, a steer-board in his skeletal hand. Aemon passed over a single golden coin before guiding us to a seat, enveloping my hand in his.

My knee bounced as the ferryman pushed off, nerves getting the better of me. What if Dad didn't approve of me anymore? He always hated the grave talker business. Now I was the Warden of Knoxville, policing arcaners as my full-time job. My ties to the human world dwindled every day, and now I was on the hunt for an ex that my father had definitely warned me not to trust.

I'd taken lives, I'd hurt people.

Was I even the little girl he raised anymore? Would he even recognize me?

"What's going on in that head of yours?" Aemon murmured into my ear, his breath tickling the skin of my neck.

I tried to still my bouncing leg, but I just couldn't manage it. "Nothing of consequence."

"Don't tell me you're bad on boats, too. I don't think Charon would like my method of distraction."

Shaking my head, I tried to paste a smile on my face. It was silly how much I wanted everything to go smoothly. How much I wanted my father to still love me, to still want me as his daughter. He'd been killed because of me. Mariana had taken his life because she knew it would hurt me.

What if he resented me for it?

My father had been gone for months, and all I thought about was what I would say to him if I ever saw him again—that was when I allowed myself to even think about him. Now that I was on my way to see him, my mind was a blank landscape of fear.

"I'm okay on boats," I whispered, hanging onto his hand for dear life. Because it wasn't the boat that was doing me in.

"He loves you, you know. Your dad. He's proud of you." Aemon dragged my bouncing legs onto his lap. "I told him you were made Warden of Knoxville. You should have seen his face. He's a good man—a good father. You got lucky in that regard."

Surprise gave way to a feeling I couldn't name bubbling inside my chest. "You talked to my dad?"

"I keep him updated when I can. I wanted to meet the man who raised you."

I couldn't tell if I was jealous or flattered. "Getting all the dirty details?"

"Of a fashion. You and Jeremiah were scoundrels in your youth, weren't you? I read most of it in your memories, but your father's recollections paint the two of you as invincible little deviants."

"We were." I shrugged at the white lie. "Still are—though neither of us are children anymore. Hell, we're not even human anymore."

We rode in silence for the trip, my head on his shoulder as the waves lapped against the hull. Our ferryman was silent, but when we docked, I still said "thank you."

"You are welcome anytime, Azrael's daughter," Charon rumbled beneath his dark hood. "I hope to see you again."

Nodding, I stepped onto the dock. "Maybe you can tell me about him sometime?"

A low, joyful chuckle came from the general vicinity of his chest. "I would like that."

My nerves got the better of me as Aemon led me through Elysium, and they reached their peak when I saw a carbon copy of the house I'd grown up in. The pretty white house was complete with the same black mailbox we'd had since I was eight. The name "Adler" was lettered neatly with our handprints on either side—his in blue and mine in purple.

Ten years ago, a group of teens had destroyed that mailbox and Dad had replaced it with a plain one. Seeing our old mailbox here and now made my heart swell.

"You think he'll—"

"Yes," Aemon murmured, cutting me off, knowing what I was going to say before I ever said it. "Killian loves you. He will always love you. Whether you are a Warden or not, whether you're—"

This time it was me cutting him off, but I did it with a kiss. "Thank you."

"Darby?" my father called from his front door, and I couldn't stop myself from sprinting across his manicured lawn and launching myself into his arms. They closed around me, and it was everything I had ever wanted all wrapped up in a bow.

"Sweetheart? What are you doing here? Are you—"

My chuckle was watery. "Dead? No. Just visiting."

He pushed me away a bit so he could look at me. The last time I'd seen him, he was bruised and bloody, his life dripping from him so fast I never got to say goodbye. Now he stood tall and whole, and I couldn't see any of it because I was crying so hard, I could barely stand up.

"I missed you," I choked out, hugging him so tight he grunted. "I missed you so much."

"I missed you, too, baby girl. So much."

He led me inside, planting me on my favorite striped chair. There were so many things I'd wanted to say to him, and I couldn't remember any of it.

And it was the best feeling in the entire world.

A cup of coffee warmed my hands as I sat curled in my favorite chair. It was a copy of the one in my dad's house on Earth, only this one didn't have the purple ink stain on it from when one of my pens exploded in tenth grade. His whole home was a copy of the one in Haunted Peak, right down to the knickknacks I'd made in my failed attempt at sculpture as a kid and some of his favorite drawings.

He could have been anywhere—on a beach sipping fruity drinks or having adventures—but his heaven was in our old house with my art on the walls and our mailbox and...

"It's good to see you again, Killian," Aemon said,

giving my father a handshake before taking the seat at my side. "Did you try the mountain climbing we talked about? I hear the view from the top is beautiful."

Mountain climbing? Dad was afraid of heights. Then again, he was already dead. What was there to be afraid of anymore?

"I did. You can see all of Elysium from up there. I enjoyed it, though, climbing without being tied in was an adjustment."

That about took me out. "You? Mister 'Don't you dare go up in that loft' himself was climbing mountains without ropes? Bullshit."

Dad gave me his censuring eyebrow for cussing, and it was so familiar and so wonderful that I couldn't breathe. How was I supposed to go back and do what I was supposed to now? How could I leave him? Did Bishop matter when I had this?

Did anything?

"Very funny. And I recall telling you not to go up in the loft because *someone* was a grade-A klutz and was known for knocking over lanterns," Dad said, but his smile was good-natured, and he was right there in front of me. "Aemon has kept me up to speed on the Warden job. Dave really took over the LeBlanc pack? And Jay?"

"He did. It's going well, too. There was some reconstruction and growing pains, but it seems like

Alpha suits him. He even seems to be balancing the pack and Captain, too. He's at peace—or as at peace as one could be, wrangling a whole pack. I figure it isn't much different than trying to keep me and Jay in line, so at least he has practice."

And Jay? How did I tell him about Jay turning into a vampire and what happened with Nero, and…

Dad chuckled as he shook his head. "I see you over there trying to gear up to tell me about Jeremiah's change. I take it you never read my letter."

My smile was brittle as I inclined my head. "Guilty. I kept it with me as long as it was safe, but could never get the gumption to read it. It's sitting in a safety deposit box in Haunted Peak First Savings Bank right now, collecting dust."

Dad crossed to me, yanking me out of my chair and enveloping me in a hug so tight, it reminded me that whatever I was, I would always be his little girl.

"I told you how proud of you I was," he whispered, swaying back and forth like he used to when I was a child. "How I thought you being Warden was a good idea and how I wanted you to break up with the Fed. I told you not to worry about Jeremiah, that he'd be safer as a vampire than anything else. That Dave would be a good Alpha. And that you should give Aemon a chance. That no matter how hurt you'd been, you deserve someone who will love you forever. Who will put you first."

Dad had tried to warn me, too... But how? "How did you know all of that? You'd died already. How—"

"Azrael paid me a visit when I was still new. I think he wanted to reassure me that you would be okay. Told bits and pieces of your future, probably knowing I'd tell you. I think he knew his end was coming soon."

"You tried to warn me about Jay."

I wish I'd have known. Maybe I'd have done things differently.

Just thinking that had me rolling my eyes at myself. I was no better than all those poor souls who begged Fate to tell them their future. This was exactly why knowing didn't do a damn thing. Me knowing what would have happened wouldn't have changed anything. Jay was always going to become a vampire. Bishop was always a bastard. Dave was always going to be the LeBlanc Alpha, and me?

You deserve someone who will love you forever. Who will put you first.

I was going to give Aemon a chance. A real one. Without thinking he was going to leave me or betray me or...

Meeting Aemon's gaze over my dad's shoulder, I let

the look he was giving me actually crack the ice around my heart.

"But you can't stay, kiddo," Dad whispered, hugging me tight before releasing me. "You have things to do, people to protect. I'm always going to be here, but you know you have to go back, don't you?"

But I didn't want to go back. Earth was hard and messy and exhausting. Elysium was easier, slower. I could breathe here. But I'd miss Jay and Jimmy and Dave and all my friends. My little family that I'd scraped together along the way. Who would protect them from Bishop? Who would stop that duplicitous maniac from stealing more power that wasn't his?

Who would put him in the ground?

"Can I visit? When this is all over, I mean? Can I... come back?"

"Of course you can. You just have things to do." He pressed a kiss to my forehead, much like Fate had. "I'll always—no matter what you have to do or who you have to kill—be proud of you. You will always be my little girl. So go handle your business, baby. I'll be here waiting for you, Darby."

Swallowing hard, I choked down the sob that threatened to erupt from my throat. I'd never gotten a goodbye on the shore of that lake, and now I knew it wouldn't have made a difference. It would always hurt to tell him goodbye.

It would always break me.

It would always break my heart.

And even now—when I knew I could see him again one day—it made me ache so bad, I didn't know how I would survive it.

But Dad was right. I had a job to do and mistakes to fix. Friends to protect. And I'd make sure he never stopped being proud of me.

I just might have to do some things I wasn't so proud of first.

13

Haunted Peak was just as hot and muggy as I remembered, and while it was good to be back on Earth, I hated it, too.

Everything moved so fast here. There was this urgency, this demand, this quickness that made it impossible to breathe. I wanted more than this. More time, more rest, more...

Just more. More than I'd ever thought to take for myself. More than I'd ever dreamed. Because it didn't have to just be work and death and pain and struggle.

Bishop La Roux wanted me to be beat down and weak and floundering. That was the reason he'd blown up Aemon's house. He wanted me off my guard and scared.

But I wasn't scared of Bishop and probably never

would be. Because he couldn't take what I wasn't ready to give up. And he'd learn that just as soon as I smoked his bastard ass out of whatever crossroads hidey-hole he'd buried himself in.

"Do you want to get some foo—" Aemon began before getting cut off by a very familiar voice that should not have startled me in the least.

Too bad it did.

"Where in the bleeding fuck have you been?" Hildy screeched, appearing in front of me like I'd fucked off to Narnia or some shit.

I barely managed to hold onto the chaos that ached to escape from my skin. Okay, so I didn't manage to hold onto any of it, and considering that we'd appeared in my backyard, every single window, my outdoor table —also glass—and all the outdoor lights exploded at once.

"Dammit, Hildy," I growled, snapping my fingers to put everything to rights. "I told you to stop doing that. For fuck's sake, man, can't you walk up like a normal person?"

The cane in Hildy's hand glowed bright as he made himself solid, a firm expression of wrath stamped all over his face.

"I asked ya where ya'd been. You'd better be tellin' me. It was bad enough you flitted off to where I couldn't follow, but I could feel ya. You went somewhere. You left this earth. Where the fuck were ya?"

Now it was me who felt like a heel. "I—"

"Did ya die? Did he bring ya back?" Tears welled in his eyes. Real tears full of anguish and regret.

"No, Hildy. I did go to the Underworld, bu—"

Hildy's whole body seemed to expand as his eyes took on that green magic.

"The Underworld?" He growled like I was a teenager that had snuck out to go to a kegger as his gaze sliced to Aemon. "You took her to the Underworld? Without a single thought to if she should go? Ya have a lot of nerve, demon."

Sighing, I put a calming hand in his, squeezing his fingers tight. "I'm a Daughter of Death, Hildy. I can come and go as I wish. We needed to hunker down and rest, and we needed somewhere Bishop couldn't follow. Considering he's hiding from Sloane and Fate, the Underworld was our best bet."

But had I known Hildy would feel me leave this earth, I would have sent him a message or something.

"I got to see Dad."

That cooled my grandfather off, his body returning to normal size as he faded back to the gray of his ghostly form. "How is the afterlife treating him?"

My smile was wobbly. "Good."

"Oh, lass. I wish it got easier, but I'm afraid it doesn't. And I'm afraid I have more bad news."

Here we go. "Aemon, how long have we been back?"

He checked his watch. "Three minutes and seventeen seconds."

That sounded about right. "Hit me with it, Hild."

"The LeBlanc pack was attacked by witches tonight. Heavy casualties."

The bottom dropped out of my gut. "Uncle Dave?"

"I don't know, lass. They haven't found him yet."

Heat raced over my skin, digging in deep as if it were yanking me across space and time. By the time I could breathe again, I was in the middle of a nearly pitch-black tunnel with rubble all around my ankles. Torches flickered in the distance, but I knew where I was.

I remembered the smell, the rot, the... the...

No, no, no. Why was I back here? Why was I in this tunnel? Why?

Did the chaos bring me to Dave? Could I help? Was Bishop lurking in the dark?

The flames of Aemon's eyes and horns appeared right in front of me along with the green magic of Hildy's cane, both the most welcomed sight in the whole damn world.

"Breathe, Flower. Just breathe," he murmured, doing his best to walk me back from a panic attack.

"Listen to your man, lass. You did good, leading us here."

A hysterical bleat of fear escaped my throat. "I-I don't know how I got here."

But I did. I did know how I ripped myself from my backyard and ended up in this tunnel. Just like when I'd gotten out of the catacombs, I'd traveled, chaos bringing me to Dave or *close* to Dave maybe. Had I not been so pissed the first time, I'd have probably been just as freaked out as I was right then.

"Your magic might know more than we do at this point, Flower. Try to call to him with your mind. See if you can locate him."

Uncle Dave had been in my life since I was in diapers. He was my father's best friend. He was my captain. He was family. And I wasn't losing any member of my family.

Not today.

Just like when I'd almost lost Aemon, that same heat boiled in my gut, churning like acid as I let it wash over me, giving into the power Shiloh had foisted onto me. I wasn't a witch. I didn't know how to cast spells. This was a magic I still didn't know how to use.

But I'd bend it to my will all the same.

The rubble at my feet vibrated with the power I didn't understand, lifting from the ground, uncovering the tunnel floor and bodies. So many bodies. Some were dead, some were close. Some wouldn't make it out of here.

"I-I can't hold it for long," I whispered. "G-get them out of here."

"I'll help her hold it for as long as I can," Hildy chimed in, his cane glowing with the stolen magic of an entire ley line.

"Just find him, Aemon," I pleaded, shoving at several tons of rock and half a damn mountain.

Fucking tunnels.

If I had my way, they'd all be banned. The whole lot of them had brought me nothing but pain and heartache. And torment. I couldn't forget torment.

A part of me had to wonder if this had been Bishop. Sure, Hildy had said it was witches who'd attacked the LeBlanc pack, but it didn't make much sense. Then again, who knew what enemies they'd had before Dave took over. I distinctly remembered his predecessor allowing some of his packmates to kill fugitive witches at some point.

It was possible I was just looking for Bishop in anything that had gone wrong.

Blood started dripping from my nose as the boulders weighed on me.

"Why don't ya try transmutation, lass? Make these

rocks feathers or dust. You're running out of steam holding them in the air like this."

I fought off the urge to kick him. Frankly, I just didn't have the energy. "You... probably could have... told me that... earlier."

You know, before my nose started bleeding, you know-it-all jackass.

Picturing the rocks in my mind, I shoved the chaos outward, begging for something as light as air. What I got was a tunnel full of sparkly hot-pink feather boas, and glitter tinsel shining off the light of Hildy's cane like a damn disco ball. Their weight was considerably lighter if not absolutely ridiculous.

"Well, that's one way to go about it," Hildy remarked as he stared at them practically floating to the ground.

"I would have preferred them not being something out of a princess party, but the job got done. Help me get rid of them, would ya?"

Because we had people to find and witches to punish, and damn if I was going to wait for that.

It took hours to clear the tunnels of people. It had taken Hildy, Aemon, and I to secure the ceilings so the whole place didn't come down on our heads, and it had used more magic than I thought possible.

By the time we'd gotten everyone out, I was more tired than I'd been in ages.

Luckily, the death toll was practically nil. I'd never been so happy to have a bunch of arcaners on the receiving end of a natural disaster in my life. There were concussions, broken bones, and more cuts and scrapes than I wanted to think about, but the deaths were fewer than I'd originally thought. The only ones were an elderly couple that could no longer shift. Their souls had left before I could even send them on, their time on Earth long over.

And Dave?

Dave was leading his pack, setting up triage tents, and ordering everyone around like I hadn't found him unconscious and bleeding not twenty minutes before. By the time the guys got there, we'd nearly gotten everyone out.

"I thought you were in Paris," Jay remarked as he walked up, his arms wide, even though his gaze laser-locked on my bloody nose.

Still, I hugged him, even though I probably should have rocketed a blood bag at his head. "Just got back."

"Hell of a welcome home," Jimmy muttered, stealing me from Jay and looking me over. "Did you get anything from Aemon's contact?"

Aemon grumbled something about vengeance, but I

just shook my head. "Yes and no. You ever hear of a Bone Fae named Edoril?"

Jimmy's eyes went wide. "Edoril is not *a* Bone Fae. He is *the* Bone Fae." His gaze sliced to Aemon. "*That* was your contact?"

So that was a yes, then. I wondered how much of a dick punch pissing him off was going to be. Considering he had betrayed us and served us up like a side of beef, it was hard to say if I cared too much about the Fae's feelings.

"What do you know about crossroads?"

Jimmy seemed confused, but it was Tobin who spoke up, sidling up beside Jimmy like he'd come from thin air, adjusting his glasses on his nose as he squinted at the tableau.

"I know to stay away from them. Dark things live in the crossroads. It makes liminal spaces look like Disneyland. If you think that's where Bishop is hiding, I guarantee he isn't having a good time."

But I had a feeling that Bishop—just like Essex before him—knew enough about the crossroads to get by.

"You should talk to Acker. He has a PhD in liminal physics and curses."

That was new information. Where would one even get a degree like that? Were there arcane universities just hanging out?

"How many degrees does Acker even have?"

"Twelve," Yazzie grumped. "Every time he gets a new one, he puts it up in his room like a shrine."

Fair enough. I had a few degrees under my belt, too, and damn, if they weren't up in my office. Those damn dissertations were brutal, I needed the evidence that I hadn't dreamt them.

"What I want to know is who did this," Jay grumped, surveying the injured wolves, and Dave directing them all like a general. "Word on the street says it was witches."

Yeah, I'd heard that bit of gossip from Hildy, too. But where was the proof?

"You think you could look in the tunnel for spell residue or sigils?"

I didn't want to point fingers if it was a regular cave-in from shoddy construction, and I really didn't want to be on the hunt for idiot witches on a vengeance kick for people who had already been arrested.

"Does this mean you're back?" Jay asked, the hope in his voice akin to a kid on Christmas morning.

Jay, Jimmy, Yazzie, and Tobin all looked at me like I held the key to happiness. "It can't be that bad with me gone."

Yazzie rolled his eyes. "The whole of Knoxville is scared shitless of you. It makes for a much easier work environment. Word got out that you were on vacation, and it has been nonstop bullshit ever since. Please, for the love of all that is holy, tell me you're coming back."

But I wasn't back. Bishop was still at large—and with a bug up his ass about the chaos he didn't have. But someone—or several someone's—could have killed Dave.

"Have a peek in the tunnel and tell me what you see, and I'll think about it."

All four of them peeled off, ready to investigate the shit out of a place I had absolutely no desire to be. Solid win.

"That was dirty, underhanded trickery, and you know it," Aemon whispered in my ear, tempering the anxiety bubbling up in my gut. "You have no intention of coming back without finishing your mission."

I knew that and he knew that, but *they* didn't know that. "Perhaps."

It didn't matter how true Aemon's words were, if it had been witches who'd brought the whole damn tunnel down on the LeBlanc pack? I might just have to moonlight for a bit.

They weren't gone for five minutes before Jay's stony expression told me everything I needed to know. It had been witches and he had proof. I knew what he was going to say, too, and damn if I was going to let him.

"No, it was not the Jacobs Coven."

But that didn't mean that they didn't know who did it.

No way was I going to let Jay go and start some shit with the biggest coven this side of the Mississippi.

This was a visit I'd have to make in person.

Goodie.

14

"Please tell me why we're here and not tucked in a bed right now," Aemon growled as I yawned for the tenth time around a breakfast sandwich.

Managing not to choke, I chewed and swallowed my food and raised a single eyebrow as I took a sip of coffee. I'd used a lot of chaos to help Dave's pack and I needed to recharge, sure, but the only way I was keeping Jay from starting an actual incident with a coven the size of a small town was to handle it myself.

Plus, Jay would cop-talk his ass into a rivalry, and I would prefer to simply ask for help.

The spelled iron gate surrounding the Jacobs property had enough banishing power in it to blow a hole in the world. Witches with this kind of juice wouldn't try to destroy a wolf pack and fuck it up. Jay was letting bias cloud his judgment.

"Because extra eyes can't hurt, and if it is Bishop doing this and not witches, I don't want to have to split my focus and chase leads that aren't there. That attack came out of nowhere, Aemon. That shit with the witches was months ago. If they were going to retaliate, it would have been then."

But if Bishop employed witches to draw me out...

I didn't say it, but I wanted to.

Thanks for Oskar. I'll remember that favor when I rip the chaos from your bones.

Bishop was out there lurking. Waiting. Watching. He could be anywhere, and that was probably the most frightening thing I could think of.

Aemon grumbled as he pressed the "Call" button on the keypad.

"State your business," a gruff voice squawked from the intercom.

"Warden of Knoxville, Darby Adler here to speak to Josiah Jacobs."

There was a slight pause. "Yeah, buddy, I know who she is. Who the fuck are you, and what are you doing here?"

Aemon's gaze found one of the gazillion cameras pointed at us. He dropped his mask, letting his demon side free. His eyes ignited, his horns grew, and a crown of fire circled his head. "Crown Prince of Hell, Aemon the Merciless. And watch your tone. We're here to speak with Josiah Jacobs. Please don't make this harder than it needs to be."

A buzzer sounded as the gate rolled back. *Well, would you look at that.*

"I should take you on all my interrogations. That was way easier."

He blinked at me, his fire eyes, horns, and crown dissolving before my very eyes. "And so you shall."

A part of me eased at that statement. Always having backup, always being within reach of him. Always making sure he was safe. We were safe. I let my shoulder bump into his as I dug another sandwich out of the greasy paper bag in his hand. Unwrapping it, we started the trek up the lane toward the house—or what I hoped was a house. The dense forest hid the majority of the structure, but I'd caught a glimpse or two of a giant roof in there somewhere.

By the time we made it to the front door of the sprawling home, I'd eaten the last five sandwiches and slurped the last of my coffee. Too bad I was still tired and hungry and there was a graveyard nearby. It wasn't close enough to drain me more than I already was, but the temptation to reap the ghosts for my own benefit was definitely there.

To be on the safe side, I saved them just in case this visit went sideways.

Josiah Jacobs' home could only be classified as a compound. Several outbuildings spoke of multiple families living on the property, but the big house appeared to have at least three wings, three floors—above ground—and enough magic juicing up the place that their coven had to be in the hundreds deep.

I just hoped they all didn't live here.

Grumbling, I smashed the doorbell with my finger, irritated that the damn door wasn't already open after the longest trek known to mankind. Seriously, if I'd have had the energy, I would have tried to snap myself there or something.

Then again, I was dog tired. I probably didn't have the juice.

A few moments later, a small blonde woman opened the door. No bigger than five-one on a good day, cornflower-blue eyes surveyed us like we were a threat, even though her smile stretched in welcome. And she was done up, too. Full face of makeup, hair in curls, her ass in slacks and a delicate top, even though it was before dawn. If someone had told me she had been a beauty queen once upon a time, I'd have believed it to my bones.

"Well, hello there, Warden. Whatever can we do for you?" She gestured for me to come in, without actually saying the words, her eyes widening a little when Aemon followed me across the threshold.

I'd had the same reaction when he'd waltzed right into my home without an invitation, but a Prince of Hell didn't need one, now did he?

"The Jacobs Coven is at your service." Her accent was thick, and her charm was enhanced with enough magic to choke an elephant, but that shit didn't work on me.

Not anymore.

She was adorable—and probably more formidable than I could fathom—but I was too damn tired for this.

"Cut the shit, cupcake. I'm tired, covered in enough dirt to fill a grave, and I'm cranky. Can I just talk to your coven leader and skip this bullshit sweetening spell work? I need a nap."

All the rest I'd gotten in the Underworld had gone up in smoke already. I was so tempted for Aemon to send us back there just so I could soak more in.

Too bad I had shit to do.

Her eyebrows rose to her hairline. "Huh. I've never met anyone that was immune before."

Aemon snorted. "Well, now you've met two. I'd suggest you do as she asks."

"Or what?" a giant of a man asked, settling himself

right behind the small woman. "Is she going to sic her demon on us?"

Aemon's smile was pure malice. "Out of the two of us, I'd be more worried about what she'd do to you, but that's your call, friend."

Oh, enough of this posturing. "For fuck's sake. We're not here to bring anyone in. We're here to ask a favor. Can we all just settle down? You're not even in my jurisdiction."

That had both of them taking a step back, their shoulders relaxing already. It wasn't the first time I'd been on the receiving end of a stonewall, but damn if it wasn't annoying.

"Well, if that's the case"—She offered her hand—"my name's Fiona. Dad is in the kitchen. Would you like a cup of coffee?"

It was five in the morning after a long night of bullshit. "I'd love one."

"Paul, go back to your post." Paul gave her a skeptical look before warning us with his gaze. Fiona rolled her eyes and led us through the massive house to an ostentatious kitchen. Tucked back in the corner was a table, and at that table, sat a man I'd been avoiding for going on six months.

Josiah Jacobs was a formidable man who could pass anywhere from forty-five to ancient. With salt-and-pepper hair—heavy on the pepper—he seemed different from his daughter in every aspect. Where she was short, he was tall. Her skin was pale, his was tan. But when she came into the room, his eyes lit up like my father's did, a soft smile tempering his severe features.

But relaxing was off the table entirely. I had no idea how old he was, but the power signature coming off the guy was off the charts, his soul so damn bright it was as if he'd chowed down on a sun or three before breakfast.

Aemon met my gaze, his chin tipping up. He felt it, too. I'd never been so happy to not have sent Jay somewhere in my life.

"Daddy, this is Darby and Aemon. They'd like to talk to you about a favor, if you're interested."

Josiah sat at a breakfast table, a knife and fork in his hands as he cut into steak and eggs. My stomach yowled in protest, and I prayed no one else heard it. A prayer dashed the second Josiah chuckled.

"Sure thing, Sugar Plum. Have Marla fix our guests a plate and get them some coffee."

Fiona nodded before peeling off so Marla could get us some food. By the smell of that steak alone, Marla was a top-notch chef, and that only made my mouth water.

Josiah pointed to the seat across from him with the business end of his steak knife. "Have a seat."

I tried not to take it as the threat it was as Aemon pulled out my chair before taking his own.

"We haven't been formally introduced, but I've heard your name enough times to feel like I know you. Darby Adler. Former homicide detective turned Warden of Knoxville. Word is you're a grave talker, but you've got to be more than that."

A giant redheaded woman swept into the room with two plates of food—one much larger than the other— and behind her was Fiona with two cups of coffee. Marla set down the large plate in front of me and the sensible one in front of Aemon. Fiona passed us our coffee before taking the seat to her father's right.

"Some people call you a demigod but that's just scuttlebutt," Fiona chimed in, looking me over with a skeptical eye.

Her words had the taste of bullshit. Whatever the word on the street was, it was a sight more than that. I ignored her leading statements to cut into my steak and pop a huge bite in my mouth. Cooked medium and spiced to perfection, the meat melted in my mouth.

What even was I anymore? Was there a demigod-plus program? What did one call someone like me?

"There's less information on you, though," she said as her gaze landed on Aemon, lying through her teeth.

Aemon snorted as he sipped his coffee. "I like to keep a low profile."

I was tempted to get up and leave, but I didn't. "I thought I told you to cut the shit. You know damn well I can taste every lie that passes your lips. I figure your minds are warded out the ass to stop him from mining everything you know, but your words are fair game. Stop dicking with me, please."

Josiah sat back in his chair, his meal forgotten. "Fair enough. We know you're a demigod, a Daughter of Death. Your sister, Sloane, is a former member of the Night Watch, and took your birth father's place. You have ties to the LeBlanc pack through their Alpha who was your adoptive father's best friend. You are the former lover of Bishop La Roux, a blood and death mage hybrid who has been excommunicated from the ABI."

Could I be called an "ex-lover" if he had to spell me? I supposed it stung only marginally less than "victim" now, didn't it?

But Josiah wasn't done.

"Your now-deceased brother, Essex Drake, was the Overseer of the entire ABI before he was beheaded a few months ago. You have ties to the Dubois nest through Ingrid Dubois and Björn Dubois by way of your childhood best friend, Jeremiah Cooper, who was recently turned. You broke up the Knoxville Coven—even though you, yourself, are technically a St. James descendant—and you dissolved the Monroe nest after they plotted in a coup that got your adoptive father killed. And you were instrumental in decimating the vampire Nero and his nest of creepy child vampires. Did we miss anything?"

"You missed some bits here and there—" *Like that Mariana was my mother and Hildenbrand O'Shea was my grandfather* "—but I'll let it slide."

I had a feeling this whole speech was supposed to be threatening, but I knew something they didn't.

"Did you know that you have bodies buried all over this property? And their ghosts live here. Now, I could go on a fact-finding mission and learn far more than I want to, or we can get to the real reason I'm here, which doesn't include me being influenced by spells"—My gaze pinned Fiona with a glare so powerful she sat back in her seat before I shifted my attention to her father— "or intimidated by someone I could kill without moving a muscle."

No wonder Jay hated this guy. If there was one thing Jeremiah Cooper despised, it was a bullshit pissing match. Chaos thrummed in my veins, aching to be let free. As tired as I was, Josiah had pissed me off enough that just by looking at him too hard, his nose started bleeding.

The color drained from his face as he wiped the blood away. I'd just drilled through all his protection, all his personal wards, and popped blood vessels without so much as a twitch.

"I have a witch problem. You're witches. I was hoping we could work together to resolve the issue without incident, but if you can't handle it, then I guess I have no use for you."

Fiona tapped the table three times, her spell pushing against my power like a toddler shoving at her parents' legs. Still, I relented.

"The LeBlanc attack. You don't think it was us?"

I rolled my eyes. "Why would it be you? You police your own, you don't cause problems, and you don't kill people who don't need killing. As far as I know, you don't participate in bullshit politics or grab more territory than you can use. How you make your money is of no concern to me as long as innocent people don't get hurt while you do it. And again, you're not in my jurisdiction."

What I didn't say was that if any of that ever changed, it wouldn't matter if they were in my jurisdiction or not, and they damn well knew it.

"I let arcaners do as they please as long as it doesn't cause me a problem. I don't get into their affairs, and they don't give me a headache. And from time to time, we all help each other out. I'm asking for a favor—

giving you a chance to police your own kind so I don't have to. We've all seen what happens when I police people."

"You planning on disbanding us, Warden? That won't go well for you," Josiah threatened, and it made me want to explode his brain all over his kitchen table.

I shifted to face Aemon. "Did he not hear a fucking word I just said?"

"Doesn't look like it." Aemon snapped his fingers and Josiah slumped in his seat, a chainsaw of a snore erupting from his nose.

Fiona startled, checking on her father, but I just sighed and ate my steak.

"What did you do to him?"

"Isn't it obvious? He's taking a nap so we can have a civilized discussion." Aemon sat back in his chair, blowing on his coffee before taking a sip. "You seem like you have a better head on your shoulders than your father—who if I may—does not give you the credit you deserve. You have a decent level of power, you're smart, and you have a better moral compass. Someone like you is wasted in a place like this."

"What's that supposed to mean?"

My chuckle was mirthless. "You're better than him. Did you just see him threatening a Daughter of Death and a Prince of Hell? All while we've come to make a deal. He's not as smart as I thought he was, which is unfortunate."

Fiona gulped. "You want us to find the witches who attacked the LeBlanc pack. We were looking into it already. Daddy didn't mean—"

"Yes, he did." I cut her off. "But since you're smarter than him, I'll do you a solid. You find whoever attacked the LeBlanc pack, and I'll forget that he just tried to threaten me to my face. Sound good to you?"

Fiona nodded fervently, her fear getting the better of her.

"Word is that it was mercenaries left over from the old Knoxville Coven. Everyone smart got the hell out of Tennessee. Daddy wouldn't take them on because of what they did—didn't want the heat, I suspect. A few stayed, settling in Ascension and Memphis and such. We heard they got paid to attack. Shouldn't be too hard to track them down. I expect we can find them within the day."

That was the glimmer of promise I felt from that girl. I had a feeling I knew who hired them, too.

"I'll be seeing you around, Fiona," I said, shoving back from the table. "You think about what I said. You're better than this, and there's more out there than just shady deals and power grabs. Promise."

Her gaze left mine as she seemed to contemplate this,

staring at her father as if she couldn't believe what she'd just witnessed.

And just to get her goat, I held onto Aemon, and we disappeared from her kitchen like her wards and protections were whittled down to nothing.

Because a healthy dose of fear never hurt.

15

I'd never been in a safe house like this.

If it wasn't the butter-soft bed linens or the incredible view, it was definitely the soaker tub that could fit my tall self along with Aemon's huge body. Plus, it was warded better than the Jacobs Coven house and no one—and I did mean no one—knew about it.

Save for the Underworld—where I couldn't go at the moment without Hildy throwing a tantrum—this was probably the only place I could get any rest.

Dave's pack was okay and now on high alert. I'd gotten word to Ingrid and the Night Watch to keep their eyes peeled and getting some shuteye was about the only thing I was good for, for about the next twelve hours. After getting clean, Aemon and I closed the curtains, curled into bed, and passed out—the incredible mountain view and sexy times with my favorite demon be damned.

So when a knock sounded at the cabin's door about five hours into my nap, to say I was pissed would be a bit of an understatement.

Bed-headed, I threw a robe over my naked ass and had a golden light sword in my hand ready to lop the head off of anyone stupid enough to wake me up.

Aemon grabbed my elbow, hauling me to a stop. I knew why, too. If no one knew about this place, then the only way they could be here was spell work, they followed us, or they were tracking us somehow. None of those things were good, and a plush robe and a light sword wasn't going to cut it in the way of a defense.

"Darby Jean Adler, open this door right now."

The light sword fizzled out in my hand as the sound of Simon's voice filtered through the door. Simon Cartwright was a member of the Night Watch and Bastian's little brother. And if he was here, something had to have gone sideways.

Also, no one knew my middle name. No one alive, anyway. What had that little shit done to glean that information?

Aemon still pulled me back, putting his body between mine and the door. Yes, he was naked under those pajama bottoms. Yes, it was sexy as hell. And yes, he opened the door with a flaming axe in his hand.

"Is it customary to just show up at a safe house you weren't invited to?" Aemon growled, staring at not only Simon, but Sarina Kenzari as well. "Because phones still work, you know."

"Tell that to your girlfriend." Sarina swept into the cabin, tossing me a duffle as she went. "You should really answer your phone if you don't want people just showing up."

"I don't even have a phone. Your ex-partner blew it up in France. With everything going on, I forgot to get a new one."

"Oh, well... It's time to get dressed. There's been an attack."

I relaxed some. "On Dave's pack? I know, I was there all night."

And it had taken thirty minutes to get all the dirt from that stupid tunnel out of my hair, too.

She sighed like her soul was trying to escape her body. "I wish. No, sweets. Ingrid's house. It was firebombed an hour ago. We would have come sooner, but we had to summon Sloane so she could tell us where you were. Every other spell to locate you wasn't working."

My gut bottomed out. *First Dave and now Ingrid?*

I gripped the duffle tighter to my chest and raced for the bathroom. Inside the bag was fighting leathers, weapons, shit kickers, and my rosaries. I slipped them over my head and got dressed as fast as I could, my brain running at warp speed.

There was no chance this wasn't Bishop. No one would target the people I loved like this—not unless they wanted to hurt me. I was still braiding my hair with the duffle over my shoulder when I barreled out of the bathroom. Luckily, Aemon was already dressed.

"Tell me what happened."

Sarina shook her head. "There isn't time. If we want to get to the evidence and specters before the ABI shows up, we need to get there and now."

Shit.

Sarina wasn't here as the ABI Director. She was here as my friend—as Ingrid's friend. And there had been casualties. A lot of them.

Nodding, I grabbed Aemon's hand. He enveloped me in his arms, spiriting me to Ingrid's home.

This wasn't the first time Ing's house had been attacked this year. Just over three months ago, ghouls had tried to kill everyone there—either as a distraction or as a way to hurt Nero's first child vampire. Ingrid had escaped him centuries ago, and as far as I knew—she'd been the only one to survive Nero's upbringing with her mind intact.

I didn't know what I thought I'd see but having Ingrid's home look like the shell of Aemon's house in France hadn't been it. My heart twisted in my chest. Jay and Jimmy sometimes stayed here. Were they okay? Was anyone alive?

I allowed myself a single moment of freaking out, and then I was back to business.

Turning to Simon and Sarina—who'd showed up three seconds after we did—I started barking orders. "I need a status report. Casualties, survivors. Do we have donors or a blood bank on standby?"

"I'll take you to Queen Dubois," Simon muttered, sharing a grave look with Sarina.

Reluctantly, I followed Simon, picking through debris and a chewed-up lawn. We circled the still-burning house, the wreckage so bad, there was no way Ingrid wasn't going to have to bulldoze the property and start over.

That was if Ingrid was still alive.

Simon was walking so slow, and he wouldn't tell me shit, and...

Fuck it.

"Mags," I called, skirting around Simon, and running

around to the back of the building. "Ingrid. Jay. Someone better start sounding off, dammit."

I caught sight of Björn coughing next to a very burned, very still body. Mags had Ingrid in her arms, her wrist at her blackened lips. The only reason I didn't fall to my knees was because my small friend's eyes were open, her blood-red irises bright against her burns as she gnawed at Mags' arm.

If I were to describe this shredding sensation in my chest, it could possibly be called helplessness. Maybe fear. Rage burned in my gut, scorching a plan of vengeance into my soul.

Several vampires were on the back lawn, some burned to ashes, their bodies withering to husks as they died. Some were only partially burned. But all I saw was Dave bloody and unconscious in that tunnel. All I saw was Ingrid and Mags nearly burned to death. Aemon's weeping skin as he struggled to breathe.

Without thinking of the consequences, I called all the souls to me, pulling them in so I could help, so I could do something besides just stand there with my thumb up my ass and pray Bishop didn't kill everyone I loved.

I saw them, even through so many different sets of eyes. There was a package—a delivery—at the door. One of the baby vamps went to get it. Hilaria. Only twenty years old, turned just four months ago. She was so proud she could walk in the day, the sun not tiring her at all.

The blood bomb took her out first, burning her to ash before she ever knew what happened.

The fire raced through the compound faster than any fire had a right to. So many were trapped. Ingrid tried to save them, but she nearly died in the trying.

Opening my eyes, they locked onto Ingrid. Even drawing on the oldest vampire I knew, Ingrid was healing slow. Too slow.

That bomb wasn't just to set fire to Ingrid's home. It was meant to kill anyone it touched. Shoving that newly claimed power out, I filled my friend with every drop her small body would take, eating away at the poison that threatened to take her mind.

I went from vampire to vampire, healing those I could, killing that damn poison before it took them all. And by the time I was done, I was sobbing on my knees in the dirt because as mad as I was, I still didn't know if Jay was okay. I didn't know if Bishop had hit anywhere else. Jay and Jimmy weren't among the dead, and I couldn't feel them, and I—

"Shh, Flower. Here." He passed over a slim phone. "Talk to Jeremiah. He's safe, love. He's safe."

Trembling, I took it, praying that it was real. That Jay was really on the phone. That this wasn't a trick. "J-Jay?"

"D?"

The breath I let out emptied my lungs. "I-I need you to engage lockdown protocol. Tell Tobin. Bug out to secondary location. Alert everyone. I'm calling in ABI backup."

Jay shouted the directions over his shoulder, the words muffled until he came back on the line. "Someone needs to watch your six, D."

And while that was true, I need him to stay safe and unharmed and fucking alive. I needed Jimmy alive, Dave, Ingrid. I needed them all safe. For a girl with so little living blood relatives, I had sure made myself a family, hadn't I?

"Get safe," I whispered. "Get safe and I'll come to you. Make sure you're doing that, and I'll let you watch my six anytime. I promise."

"Liar," he shot back.

Being friends as long as we had, he knew me better than anyone. He knew that protecting him and Jimmy had always been my job. It didn't matter that he was a vampire now. It didn't matter that he could heal. Bishop knew everything about me—probably even things I never remembered telling him. He knew Dave and Jimmy and the rest of my friends were my weak spot.

I had a lot of fucking weak spots.

"Don't open any packages. Just leave, you got me?

Don't grab anything. Just go. Take the boys with you. Give my love to Jimmy."

And then I hung up on my best friend in the entire world and hoped that he listened to me just this once.

"Someone get me Lise Dubois. I want her here. Now."

Someone had to deal with the blood curse her grandson had wrought. Someone needed to answer for his crimes. And if there was a spell to be done, I'd need his familial blood to do it.

"She's already on her way, Flower. But there's something else you need to see."

Unless it was a fountain of magic that kept everyone I loved safe, I couldn't see me having a need for any of it.

A hundred yards away in the middle of a patch of cut-up grass was a catatonic shifter with a knife in his hand. The knife was covered in dirt, clutched so tightly to his chest as he laid in the grass, it was a wonder the handle hadn't broken off.

And he smelled wrong.

He smelled of magic and poison and...

There was a delivery. *Someone* had to have delivered the blood bomb. Someone had to have done Bishop's bidding. And Bishop La Roux was damn good at making people do what he wanted.

"I'd bet everything in my piggy bank he belongs to the

LeBlanc pack," I muttered, staring at the poor soul who'd been spelled out of his mind.

Then again, this was Bishop we were talking about. He could be a blood bomb himself. He could be an assassin, a kidnapper, a Typhoid Mary. The possibilities were endless.

I needed Lise Dubois here now.

"Get your hands off of me," the woman in question screeched, her French accent thicker than I'd remembered as she tried to get her arm out of Simon's hold.

Eyes black and grip tight, he marched her right to me before dropping her like he was being burned.

"You insidious little bitch," he growled, staring at a burn on his hand. "You'd better fix this before I make your day far more uncomfortable than it already is."

"You stole me from my home, mage. Why would I not burn you?"

Simon stepped closer, like he'd really enjoy punting her into a volcano or something. "And I told you there was an emergency with your bleeding progeny. E-mer-gen-cy." He sounded out the syllables as if she were slow. "It means I can't explain and you're just going to have to trust me. Not all death mages are like your grandson. Would you like to see what your precious grandson has done?"

Simon gestured to the shifter and the house and piles of ash and vampire husks. "And if you'd like proof, why don't you have a look at the note he made that shifter leave."

I hadn't been able to make myself read it.

Because it was pretty clear what Bishop wanted.

I told you we weren't done. You can end this when you give me what I want. Don't make me ask again. –B

This was asking? I'd hate to see what demanding was like.

Bishop wanted the chaos that Shiloh had given to me —chaos I hadn't asked for but received all the same. He wanted to strip it from my bones, and he was going to use any means necessary to get it.

"I don't know what he has on you," I growled under my breath, not bothering to look at the council leader as she surveyed the note carved in the lawn. "And frankly, I don't care. You're giving your blood so we can find him."

I was about to conjure a blade from thin air and cut her myself when Aemon's phone went off in my hand. The name "Aldrich Tobin" flashed across the caller ID, and I answered it without even a second thought.

When I picked up, the line was rife with static, but a few seconds later, I heard something that made my knees nearly give out.

"C-castle has f-fallen. S-send he-help."

Tobin and I had come up with those code words after the Warden house had been attacked by Nero. My friend had nearly died after the attack, trying to warn us that it wasn't safe to enter.

If the castle had fallen, it meant that they were overrun. That there was a trap sprung.

That we'd be walking right into it.

And even though I had come up with that damn code and knew exactly what it meant, I didn't give a single fuck that I was walking right into where Bishop wanted me to be.

Because Bishop La Roux had hurt my friends for the last time.

16

"Get everyone who can stand. Warden house. Now."

My barked command had a bit of chaos on it, drilling into every ear within a five-hundred-foot radius. Those who couldn't travel with us needed to get their asses in gear.

At Lise's startled squawk, the blade of golden light formed in my hand. It was at her throat before she could move an inch. I didn't like the head of the council any more than I liked her predecessor, but I needed her alive.

For now. Or unless she became a problem.

"You're either helping or your head will be on this lawn before you can think of a spell to cast. Understand?"

Her wide red eyes were such a contrast to her pale

skin and dark hair. They reminded me of Ingrid. Of Mags. Of how ancient she was. Of how many vampires could call her grandmother.

And I would end her without a second thought, I didn't give that first fuck who her progeny was.

"You misunderstand me. My daughter's son has gone too far. I will assist you in finding him. But I will not spill familial blood—the curse that holds is one I cannot bear. If you want him dead, you must do it yourself."

I could agree to those terms. "Fine."

My sword disappeared. "Fix that shifter and follow us. We'll need you. Yes?"

Lise gave me a jerky nod, her red eyes focusing on the catatonic shifter. I had a feeling I knew what pack he belonged to, and what that might mean, but I couldn't focus on that right then.

"You know we're walking into a trap, right?" Aemon growled under his breath, his steps matching mine as we stalked closer to Mags and Ingrid. "I'm not going to stop you, I just—"

I stuttered to a stop, pressing a quick kiss to his lips. "I know what I'm walking into. You can stay if you w—"

Aemon's mouth crashed onto mine, cutting off whatever bullshit that I was about to come up with. "I'm not letting you go alone. Not ever. I just want to do this smart."

But there was no way to do this smart. Bishop had seen to that. If we waited and scoped the place out, people could die. If we came in guns blazing, people could die. There was no smart way to play this—there were no good options.

Only bad ones.

"We're coming with you," Ingrid croaked, her skin sallow but she was upright.

Her hair was growing back in patches and her glitter sneakers were nowhere to be found, but she seemed determined to stand on her own two feet—Mags' disapproval be damned. Mags herself was worried, torn. She had too many lost to Bishop's scheming, and she'd nearly lost her enforcer. Yes, Ingrid was more than that, but...

"I think it's high time you called Sloane," Simon suggested, offering my small vampire friend his hand. "Everyone take hold. This will be a quick trip."

But I didn't have to tell my sister anything. She knew exactly where I was and what I was doing. And I couldn't say I'd want to see her in the middle of a battle. Seeing Death in the middle of a fight usually spelled bad things.

Ingrid, Mags, Björn, and Sarina held onto Simon as I placed my hand into Aemon's. When the smoke cleared, a part of me wished I would have prepared better— brought more weapons.

Because it wasn't just the dead ghoul bodies littering the lawn or the fire blazing in the front room or the glass blown out of every window. It was the smell of blood and bile and spent magic and ozone. And worse?

It was the silence.

The stillness.

The death.

And I had no desire to call the souls to me. Because I didn't want to know if my friends were among them. Not yet. I wanted to stop time altogether. I wanted to not know. I wanted just a few more seconds of ignorance.

But Bishop would never let me rest, never let me have even a second's peace.

I hadn't taken two steps before I felt the shift. Just like before Aemon's house blew, there was almost a shimmer on the air, the faint vibration of magic igniting, and I knew just what I was walking into.

Chaos took over, stealing control as the explosion rocked the earth. Because I didn't run or fall down or get blown off my feet. Instead, that power rose in me, blanketing the house as it threatened to blow apart. Fire licked at the chaos, fighting to reach out, to run free, to spread Bishop's poison through the whole neighborhood.

But I wasn't going to let it free. No, I stole it for my own, sucked it in, absorbing every bit of energy and magic, siphoning the destruction into myself. It was like pouring gasoline on a bonfire.

I felt the poison of the curse, the salt added to the bomb, the fire and debris and the death in it. He hadn't just meant to kill me and my friends. He'd meant to kill Aemon, too. He'd meant to murder every single person I cared about and steal my magic for his own.

Chaos burned through the curse like it was tissue paper, the blood poison fading away to nothing, but the rest? It had to go somewhere. There was no holding onto destruction like this. Knocked to my knees, I tried to push it up, away, far from the homes and the trees, but there was little I could do besides pray I didn't blow up.

A scream ripped up my throat as the fire tore from my skin, the blast knocking everyone away from me. The blaze shot up in the sky, turning the night into day for a brief moment before dying away.

"What in the blue bloody fuck was that?" Simon groaned, peeling himself off the pavement like I'd personally body-slammed him or something. Considering I was still trying to breathe, I didn't answer him, favoring forcing air into my lungs over quenching his curiosity.

Aemon's response was a tad bit gruffer. "She saved everyone's life, you bumbling halfwit. Show some fucking respect."

If I could have breathed, I would have laughed, but all I could manage was rolling on my side and reaching for him. He took my hand, pulling me onto his lap. "You did so well, Flower. You saved us."

But I didn't give a shit about me. There was so much salt in that bomb. So much poison. Bishop had meant to kill everyone—not caring a whit about what war he'd start in the trying.

"Help me up," I croaked. I needed to see for myself if my guys were... if they were... Alive? Broken? Breathing? "I need to get in there."

Aemon's mouth thinned, but he nodded, pulling me to my feet. He helped me walk over ghoul bodies, over broken glass, and destroyed furniture. The structure itself was unstable, the bomb doing far more damage than I could repair. The stairs were in splinters, with no clear paths anywhere.

Sarina took the lead, directing us to Yazzie who was stuck under a header that had collapsed. Blood poured from his head, his shifter healing doing nothing to slow it down. Björn, Aemon, and Simon worked together to get him free, yanking the big man out of the rubble.

"I need to get up there," Ingrid croaked at my elbow, her voice still like broken glass, even though her hair had fully returned, and her skin was no longer hamburger. "I don't trust anyone else to not bring this whole place down on our heads."

Ingrid was no bigger than an eight-year-old, and the only one of us who might have a chance at not disturbing the fragile structure.

Using Aemon as a springboard, my small friend vaulted to the nearly destroyed landing, her touchdown light as a feather. Still, I felt every thump of her feet and every breath as she moved from room to room.

When I saw her fully healed face over the edge of the destroyed railing, I knew she'd come up empty.

And that's when my heart decided to slither out of my body.

"Where the fuck are they?" I growled under my breath, shoving through debris to the kitchen. There was nothing but an upturned fridge and an open back door. The back courtyard was littered with bodies. Headless ghouls withered to husks on the cobblestones, their black blood staining the lawn in great arcs of sword strokes.

Then there were others, their necks ripped clean off.

Jimmy and Jay.

But even though their handiwork was here, *they* weren't here. All I found was Acker huddled against the house with Tobin on his lap. My heart dropped as the scent of his blood filled my nose. Tobin's middle was damn near gone, his face the white of the nearly bloodless. He struggled to take in air, his breaths coming in these awful, shocky pants as he stared at nothing.

"I-I don't know what to do. I don't know what to do," Acker whispered, hanging on tight to his friend as his wide eyes met mine.

I didn't either. Tobin was so far gone—just like Jay had been in that fucking tunnel—that I knew helping him would only kill me. Unless we got a miracle, there was nothing I could do.

And that fucking killed me.

Mags appeared at my left, her dark hair windswept and red eyes shining like a mirage in the desert. "Give him to me. I will help your friend."

Acker clutched Tobin closer to him, the thin man moaning in pain as he did so. It was as if Acker thought if he held Tobin tighter, he would keep him alive somehow.

"Fear not, Ambrose," Mags cooed, caressing Acker's face like a lover. His face softened in the trance of her voice, her compulsion calming him a fraction. "Your friend agreed to the covenant ages ago just as Jeremiah had. I will save him, I promise you."

Reluctantly, Acker released Tobin and the slender woman pulled the tall man into her arms like he weighed no more than a baby. And just like she'd done to Ingrid, she sliced her wrist wide, feeding him her blood. At first,

Tobin didn't take the blood, too far gone to realize what was happening. But the first swallow changed his tune. And as he drank, his eyes bled from green to red as the change began.

Tobin shredded Mags' arm, talons erupting from his fingertips. The sharp nails cut into her skin, but she didn't so much as flinch. No, she brushed his sweaty mop of curls away from his forehead as she clutched him closer, curling around her new progeny in an almost loving embrace.

I'd never seen someone changed over—heard about it, sure—but never seen it. Never seen the bond formed or the care in which Magdalena gave to her nest.

Mags looked up at us. "He will live," she assured me, her smile confident as Tobin's drinks became more ravenous. "Do not worry about this one. I have a feeling he will be formidable when he rises."

But I would worry about Tobin. I'd worry about everyone. And that still didn't tell me where the fuck Jay and Jimmy were.

"Ambrose, tell me what happened," I ordered, but Acker was staring at Tobin and Mags, the hint of fear and jealousy warring on his face. Acker was a Mormo—bound, of course—but the lust was still there.

I didn't want to do it, but I still slapped the shit out of him to snap Acker out of it.

He sucked in a breath, finally focusing on me. "Thanks. I need to up my bonds, I think. Too many blood drinkers in the house."

"We'll get right on that just as soon as you tell me what happened. Where are Jay and Jimmy?"

Acker shook his head, his red-brown eyes wide like he didn't want to tell me what had transpired here today. "I don't know. I—it all happened so fast. Y-you told C-cooper to bug out and we were. Tobin ne-needed his hard drives, but we were headed to a safe house when the ghouls came. Th-there were so many. Yazzie, Cooper, and Hanson, they took a lot of them out, but—"

Aemon latched onto Acker's arm, a faint tendril of smoke curling around his hand like a snake. "You're safe now, Ambrose. No one will hurt you. Aldrich will get better, and Yazzie is awake. We just need to know what happened to Cooper and Hanson. You can tell us. It's safe."

Like Mags' compulsion, Aemon's power relaxed the agent enough that his shoulders climbed out of his ears and the shock faded some.

"A ghoul bit Cooper. One second, they were cutting them down and then Hanson got cut. He was okay, but Jay, he flew into a rage. He wasn't paying attention. One of the ghouls got too close. I think it was poison—the bite, I mean. It happened so fast. Cooper started clawing at his skin. And he was screaming, saying that Hanson should stay away, that he was thirsty. He took off and Jimmy followed."

Ambrose swallowed. "I don't know where they are."

Sarina sidled up, her gaze a far-off quality that meant she was seeing things that might come to be.

"You don't, but I do."

I just hoped we didn't get there too late.

17

Sarina was a human-sized GPS, riding shotgun in Jimmy's totally stolen and magically hot-wired Suburban. Unfortunately, Jay was getting fuzzier and fuzzier to my oracle friend, so we were winging it. The northbound lanes of Interstate 75 were a nightmare, but trying to leapfrog through visions just wasn't going to work. There wasn't more to go on than a direction and a prayer we were following the right one.

"Left or right?" I asked as we headed for the stoplight leading into Haunted Peak. If there was one place Jay might go, it would be home.

But that could mean his mother's house, the house he'd purchased next to mine when we'd graduated from college, or anywhere in between. I prayed to every deity I knew of that he went to his empty house instead of his mom's. Mrs. Cooper was still in the dark about all this arcaner bullshit and the last thing we needed was her finding out her son was a vampire the hard way.

Sarina rubbed at her temple, shaking her head. "It's like a damn kaleidoscope in his brain right now. He can't think straight. I don't know—"

Losing patience—if I'd ever had it—I refused to wait for an answer. Punching it, I turned right into town, hoping I knew my best friend's mind—even if said mind was clouded by a blood curse. I wished for a siren as I blew through town, and when I made it to Jay's house, I barely put the truck into park before jumping out.

In the back of my mind, I knew Aemon, Simon, Sarina, and Ingrid were following me, but all I saw was evidence we were probably in the right place.

Jay's front door was in splinters, half-hanging off its hinges, the wood streaked in fresh blood.

Oh, shit. Please be here. Please be here.

Carefully, I eased into the house, wishing for a gun or something. If it came down to it, taking Jay's head was about dead last on the list of things I ever wanted to do. His living room was a wreck. The couch was in two pieces, the coffee table shattered. The artwork was off the walls, slashed to ribbons. A body-sized hole was in the drywall, revealing a demolished bedroom, the hallway no better.

But instead of finding Jay in his house, all we found was Jimmy on the other side of the island propped against the dented cabinets. Breaths sawing through his lungs, eyes wide, pupils blown with shock, he clutched at his face as blood seeped through the cracks in his fingers. Sword in hand, he tried to raise it, but his arm was damn near destroyed.

And that said nothing about his chest.

Wide-open wounds wept scarlet blood, his royal-blue shirt soaked in it.

I'd been protecting Jimmy Hanson since I was a kid. Quiet, shy, and oh, so small as a child, he got picked on incessantly. Jay and I had always kept the bullies away. Always. As he aged the bullies dwindled, but he'd always been under my protection. It didn't matter if he was a certified giant or how deadly he was with a blade.

Now it felt like I was eight years old again, watching Jimmy try and stem a bloody nose. I'd been helpless then, and I was helpless now.

"I-I lost him, Darby. I lost him," Jimmy's clear blue eyes were filled with tears as he struggled to suck in air. "He was so fast, I could barely keep up. He didn't mean it. I know he didn't mean it."

He tried to get up, but his legs wouldn't hold his weight, sliding in his own blood.

"Easy, mate," Aemon murmured when I couldn't say

anything for fear of bursting into tears. "We'll fix you right up."

Jay did this to him. *Jay.* The man who swore no one would ever hurt him. Who'd protected Jimmy since we were kids. The man who loved him to distraction, who would do anything for him.

Jeremiah did this. He's killed him. Oh, god. He'll never forgive himself.

"Tell me what happened," I urged, taking the sword out of Jimmy's hand and replacing it with my own, squeezing tight.

Jimmy's gaze met mine, the fear and pain in it nearly bottoming out my stomach. "I was stupid. I thought I could protect him. I could smell the curse in their blood. I knew it was bad. I got sloppy. A ghoul got me with his blade. And Jay... he lost it. Vamped out, went feral. He-he tried to get me out of there. A ghoul bit him. Tobin tried to help. He got in the way and..." Jimmy tried to get up again, but he was losing too much blood.

"He was the one to hurt Tobin, wasn't he?" I offered, giving Jimmy just a little bit of myself, praying it was enough. Jimmy was Fae, unless Jay had gotten him with iron, he should have been healing already. "Tobin got too close after he was infected, right?"

I felt the curse in his blood. That ghoul's blade must have been laced with it. Shoving more of myself into him, I breathed a tiny sigh of relief when the damn spell broke. The deep gashes in Jimmy's arm and chest started to close, but I couldn't give him much more without passing out. My nose was already starting to bleed.

"He didn't mean it. He tried to stop. Please don't kill him. Please." Jimmy latched onto me, begging me not to kill my best friend on the whole planet. "He didn't mean it. I swear."

I fought off the urge to thump him on the forehead. The man was damn near dying, after all. "Tobin is going to be fine, Jimmy. And I'm not going to kill Jay. I just need to know where he is."

Jimmy shook his head. "A-after he..." He trailed off, his mouth twisting in torment. "He took off. Said he wasn't going to hurt anyone ever again. I tried to follow him, but..."

I brushed the blood off my upper lip, trying not to scream. Jay told me after he turned, if he ever hurt Jimmy, he'd never forgive himself. I had an ugly feeling in my gut that I knew exactly what Jimmy was saying.

"He tell you where he was going?"

How I sounded calm, I had no idea. It felt like my heart was getting ripped out of my chest.

Once again, Jimmy shook his head. "You have to stop him, Darby. Please."

"I will. I swear to you. I'll—"

But how could I stop my best friend from doing something so fucking stupid if I didn't know where he was? I was making a promise I wasn't sure I could keep.

Shaking, I met Aemon's fire eyes. His thumb brushed the blood away from my lip, his rage filling the room.

I was weak. Small. I wasn't strong enough. Even with all the chaos. Even with the remnants of the souls from the catacombs. I wasn't strong enough to fully heal Jimmy. I wasn't strong enough to get to Jay.

"Get mad, Flower," Aemon ordered, his power filling me in little sips. "Focus that chaos. Bishop poisoned your best friend. He hurt your family. He nearly got Tobin killed. And if you don't get mad now, Jeremiah is going to kill himself. You know it and I know it. So, get mad, Darby. Now."

Heat threaded through me, burning through my gut and into my fingers and toes. Every word out of Aemon's mouth was true. I was strong enough. I'd gone to Dave before, I'd gotten out of the catacombs.

I could do this.

Picture him. See him. Where is he?

Fire raced over my skin until a familiar ripping sensation yanked me by the middle across space and time, stealing my breath. By the time I could suck in air again, my knees were in silty sand as water lapped at my fingertips.

My eyes could barely focus, and it wasn't until I heard the sounds of a struggle did the scene in front of me even become clear.

Jay had a stake in his hand, and he was desperately fighting against Hildy to shove it into his own heart. Hildy was incorporeal, hanging onto that fucking tree branch of a stake for dear life while he cussed a blue streak.

"Ya fecking idjit. If I didn't love my granddaughter so fecking much I'd let ya ram that blasted stake right up yer ass. Stop fighting me, ya miserable wanker." Hildy yanked the stake out of Jay's hold, tossing it into the lake.

He tried to tackle Jay, but his magic could only do so much while he was still ghosty, and Jay was determined. Jay raced for the stake, getting to it before even Hildy could catch up with him.

"I ought to snap your bleeding neck, you blithering idiot."

But Jay didn't say anything back. All he did was sob as the blood curse tried to take him over. "I can't hurt anyone else," he roared. "I killed them. Can't you see that? I killed him. Oh, god, James." Jay landed on his knees, the stake gripped so tight in his hands it nearly shattered. "I'm so sorry. I'm so sorry, baby. I didn't mean it."

This was what Bishop had done. He'd taken a good

man and brought him low. He'd torn his whole life apart. Twice. First when he killed Jay, and second when he nearly made him murder his love.

And Jay... I was so fucking mad at him, I wanted to scream.

Instead, I shoved to my feet, racing for my best friend in the world like I'd been shot from a cannon. Jay saw me, too. He saw me coming for him. He saw me trying my best to keep him alive.

And I got to watch Jay drive that stake into himself.

Light exploded out of me as I screamed, my power focused on one thing, and one thing only. That spark of chaos burned that stake to ash. Whether or not it did it in time was the real question. Before I could stop myself, I'd tackled Jay to the ground. We rolled in the sand before his shoulders were embedded into the beach.

Without much thought on my part, I checked to make sure he was still breathing, that the damn wood hadn't pierced his heart.

Did I care that he was scratching at me with his talons?

No. No, I did not.

Because if he could scratch me, he was fucking well alive.

And once I ascertained he was indeed breathing, I reared back and punched him as hard as I could in the jaw. The bone snapped like a twig, and I probably shattered his cheekbone, but damn, if the fucker wasn't knocked out.

Rolling off of him, I sucked in huge gulps of air as my back hit the sand. But I couldn't stay still, I was so fucking mad, it was like ants were in my limbs. Pacing like a damn lion, I stared at my best friend on the planet and fought off the urge to kick him in the balls.

"Lass?" Hildy crooned, but I couldn't look at him.

All I wanted to do was scream. Did he really think I would let Jimmy die? That Sloane would take him from us? Did he not for one second think it through? After all I'd done, after all I'd sacrificed, he thought he was just going to "stake" himself out of my life? What the fuck.

"Darby, girl, can you look at me?" Hildy begged, and I did briefly before continuing my pace.

"How?" I barked, my jaw like granite. "How could he do this to me? I damn near died trying to keep him in the world and he hauls off and does this shit. If I didn't love him so damn much, I would kill him. I would rip out his heart and fucking eat it in front of him before his light went out."

Sand whirled around us, and the water crashed onto the shore. The wind whipped through the trees as mounds of fire fell from my feet as I paced, and by the way, I didn't give a shit about any of it.

"You're my brother, you fucking idiot," I yelled at Jay's very unconscious body, resisting the urge to kick him again, but only barely.

"You think I won't go to the Underworld and fucking rip you out of it? You think I won't barter, beg, and steal to keep you breathing? You don't get to die on me, you selfish motherfucker. You fucking don't. Not you."

It was like I was in that tunnel all over again. It was like I was watching that wolf attack him. Watching him tear his throat open. It was like my hands were still covered in his blood. It was as if I was still holding his throat together. It was as if I was dying in the dark, praying he had a good life without me in it.

It was as if I was watching Dad's light leave him.

A gentle hand touched my shoulder, but I flicked it off.

"Flower?" Aemon cooed, but the nickname made me want to scream.

"Don't you dare call me Flower right now, Aemon," I seethed through gritted teeth. "You don't get to handle me. In fact, I dare someone to come up here and try and talk me down. I get to be mad. And I'll be as mad as I want to be until Lise Dubois comes down here herself and fixes what her grandson broke."

Aemon's wide eyes took me in, and I couldn't tell if he was scared or turned on. I would have preferred the former, but I had a feeling it was the latter. "Did you know you're bleeding?"

Did I know that Jay had scratched me to hell and back? Yes, I sure as shit did. Jay had cut all the way through my leathers, and damn if I was going to look. But until I could get stitches or a whole host of souls in me, I was shit out of luck in that department.

"Yes," I hissed, "I'm aware."

"Are you also aware that you have set the entire beach on fire?"

Aemon's smile made me want to punch him. Because no doubt he thought this was an adorable little tantrum I was having. But while I was aware there was something more happening, the whole beach hadn't quite made it into my consciousness until right then.

"Maybe. What of it?"

Aemon crossed his arms over his chest and gave me another "too cute for his own good" grin. "I'd love to have Lise visit with Jeremiah, but she can't get to him if the beach is on fire. Since I'm the only one who is fireproof— besides you, evidently—I've been selected as the sacrificial lamb to get you to stand down. Cooper will only be asleep so long, Flower."

There he went calling me Flower again. But I was still so fucking mad at Jay. So mad I couldn't see straight. "He tried to leave me, Aemon. He was going to... he was..."

I couldn't even finish that sentence. Saying it out loud made me want to bawl.

Risking my wrath, Aemon closed the distance between us, wrapping an arm around me and pulling me against his front.

"But you stopped him, didn't you? You fixed it. And as soon as Cooper realizes he didn't kill the love of his life, he'll understand just what you went through to keep him breathing. I know you're angry and I know I told you to get mad, but the job's done, love. It's time for you to let it go. If you don't, it'll only poison you in the end."

But it wasn't time to let it go. Instead, I'd just have to shove it down, cover it up, pull it away from prying eyes until my friends were trying to die on me.

Oh, so slowly, I pulled the flames into myself, praying chaos didn't fuck me over as I absorbed it all. But shoving that anger down had consequences. For one, the pain from Jay's mauling finally registered, the white-hot agony *abso-fucking-lutely* rearing its ugly head.

Looking down, I saw the wide-open gashes on my arm and middle. The rips in my thighs. Bile rose as I tore my gaze away, but the world tilted.

Hard.

"Motherfu—"

But I was pretty sure I didn't finish that curse before I was dead to the world.

18

The last time I woke up in a cemetery, I had been possessed. Aemon had been trying to get me to set him free and had taken me over after the first night of real sleep I'd gotten in days.

This time wasn't much different. Aemon had still taken me to a cemetery, but it was for a very different purpose.

"Olly, Olly oxen free," he called while cradling me on his lap, his voice a touch sad for some reason. "Come out to play, wee little ghosties. I promise I won't bite."

Sure. Because ghosts just wandered up to Princes of Hell every day. No specter would go within a mile of Aemon or any other demon if they were smart.

"It's like you've never called a soul to you in your

life," I croaked, cracking an eyelid. "You know I hate cemeteries, Aemon. Why—"

He crushed his lips to mine for a brief moment before giving me a look that could peel the paint off a car. "You have been unconscious for an hour. Something is wrong. You're not letting me heal you anymore. Hildy tried, too, but he could only give you so much. The chaos just isn't accepting it. I thought we were going to lose you."

"So, you thought a cemetery full of ghosts and she'll heal right up?" I jeered, trying to sit up. My wounds smarted, but at least they were closed. "You sure I don't have a blood curse on me or something?"

Aemon's grip got tighter before he let me right myself. "I don't know. You don't smell like you have one on you, but I couldn't scent Hanson or Cooper's until after you broke them. I don't like this, Flower. I need you healed. You not taking my power? I fucking hate it."

Gently, I rested my forehead against his. "I know how you feel."

And I really, really did. Outside the catacombs, I'd thought I was going to lose him. I'd thought he was going to die right in front of me and I—

"I'll get better. Promise."

But sitting up was starting to suck. Maybe calling souls *was* a good idea. Focusing all my energy on finding souls willing to cross physically hurt. Everything hurt.

One timid specter moved close, an elderly man. He had a sweater vest and a cane, his left foot dragging a little as he walked, even though he didn't need to walk anymore. But he seemed more concerned with the demon at my back than the fact that I couldn't even stand up.

"Are you here to take me to Hell, child?" he asked, not quite fighting the pull anymore.

My chuckle was mirthless. "I don't decide where you go. But if you're worried about the demon, don't. If you're not an asshole, he's practically a pussy cat."

That was a total lie, but reassuring the man seemed more prudent than the truth.

He chuckled, eyeing Aemon like he knew I was full of shit. "I doubt that. You seem hurt. Can I help or—"

He drifted closer, his name coming to me just like snippets of his life. Neil had been to war and back, the scars tainting his mind more and more as he aged. But there hadn't been much treatment for PTSD back then, so he'd left his wife and kids, worried that one day his nightmares would get the better of him and he'd hurt them. He died alone. No wife. No kids. No friends. Afraid he'd damage them as he had been.

"It's okay, Neil. I know a very nice lady you should talk to when you get to Elysium. Her name is Sloane.

She's my sister. She'll take good care of you. You'll tell her I said 'hey' won't you?"

"I-if you're sure. I... I killed people over there. I always wondered what would happen... if I'd go to Hell or not."

But it was Aemon who reassured him this time. "Hell was not meant for people like you. I should know, I help run it from time to time. Now, hop along. Your family is waiting for you."

"Here," I prompted, offering him my hand. "It won't hurt."

Neil reluctantly put his hand in mine as I tugged at his soul. Instantly, it was like taking a breath that I'd been holding too long. Air filled my lungs, the stitch in my side that I hadn't noticed gone. The places Jay's talons had gotten me healed a bit more, the muscles and sinew knitting back together at a faster rate.

Now that dying was off the table, I tottered to my feet. Nope, one soul wasn't going to do it.

"You need more, Flower. Call more to you."

At Aemon's urging, I did. I pulled more souls—more than I had before in this cemetery. It made me think that Sloane left the ones in this town just for me. All told, there were five that I took, the majority good ones with nice souls that didn't make me want to throw up. But there was one that made it almost hurt to take, his memories viler than I wanted to see.

"I've taken enough," I insisted, but that wasn't true. I still didn't feel right. "Take me back to Jay. I want to make sure Lise does her job."

On the off chance that blood curse infected me, too, I'd need her to fix what her bastard of a grandson broke.

A moment later, we were back at the blackened shore of Whisper Lake, and I got a good look at my destruction. There was one thing about chaos: it sure as hell went off on a tangent when it got going. Not only was the sand damn near solidified into glass, but the houses that had once graced the shore were now blackened husks.

Covering my mouth, I asked the question I feared most of all. "Did I kill anyone?"

I'd only ever killed out of necessity, out of self-preservation. Never on accident, never out of rage.

"No, Flower. These houses have been abandoned since the coven left Tennessee. Other than shattering Jeremiah's jaw, you didn't hurt anyone."

Wincing, I looked around for my best friend, who I found still unconscious with Ingrid and Sarina sitting on his chest. He roused a little bit, nearly bucking them off before my tiny vampire friend hauled back and socked him in the temple. Unconscious once more, I had a feeling this routine would only work for so long.

Plus, I had a definite concern about brain damage.

"Remind me to never piss you off," Simon said before letting out a low whistle, his feet crunching in what used to be sand. "You know, Bastian told me you were like this, but damn if I believed him. He said you were the most frightening thing he's ever seen, and he was dating Death herself."

Simon was one to talk. I'd heard stories about his exploits from Sloane, and if there was any death mage I was really glad that was on my side, it was Simon. The shit Simon was capable of made Bishop look like a fucking clown.

"Married. He's *married* to Death herself," I croaked, spilling the beans good and proper. It was better for him to find out from me, instead of throwing a hissy fit like I had. I wanted Sloane and Bastian to have a happy reaction the next time they told someone.

Simon took a step back like I'd socked him in the gut. "Married? Good of him to invite me to the wedding, that wanker."

"See? That's what I said. It's bullshit. 'We just put on the rings and decided to be married.' I'm still mad about it."

But that was a little too much exertion because a cough racked my chest, and I knew I was in deep shit because my hand came away red.

Not good.

"Umm, we got an ETA on Lise?" I asked, showing Simon and Aemon my now-bloody hand.

Aemon clutched me to him tighter, his eyes blazing with his demon. "You didn't take enough. You—"

I let my forehead touch his. "There was never going to be enough for me to take. I've been poisoned, cursed. It's not letting me heal. You know that."

Even when Aemon was dying, I'd never seen him look as helpless as he did right then. "Your sister had better stay away from you, got it? She's not taking you—not right now."

"I'll get her," Simon mumbled, disappearing in the closest shadow before appearing barely a few seconds later with the blood mage in tow.

"For the last time, unhand me," Lise growled at Simon, burning the hand that held her bicep.

Simon's pale eyes turned black. "And just like last time, I told you it was an emergency."

"Everything to you children is an emergency. 'He's dying, she's in trouble.' It is all the same. This urgency whe—"

Aemon stood with me in his arms, his fire eyes and horns and crown barreling down on Lise before she could even get her bearings, her tirade forgotten.

"Maybe you should hold your tongue, yes?" he

growled, the implied threat of cutting it out of her head unspoken but very real. "You will heal her, understand? There is no 'try' for you. You will break whatever magic your grandson has wrought, or I will make you pay. Personally."

There were a few times where I had seen Lise Dubois frightened, and all of them involved Aemon. Face whiter than a ghost and eyes wider than saucers, she nodded like she was being scolded by the principal. Considering out of everyone I knew, Aemon—save for his father—was the oldest by far, it was probably exactly like being sent to the office.

A cough hit me again—a wet, bloody one that made me feel like my insides were rotting. *Joy.*

"Anytime, mage."

"Y-yes. Of course, I will help."

Then she broke off in rapid French, which I still didn't understand. I really should have done that language matrixing spell Sloane told me about. I caught "sister" and "blood" and not much else.

Sloane. I think they need you. I think... I think I might be dying a little bit. If it won't piss Fate off too bad, do you think you could come help? I know I said I wanted to see my dad more, but...

The thought was barely in my head before Sloane

DEAD & BURIED ● 209

appeared on the shore, scythe in hand, wings outstretched. She came alone, and I figured that was a very bad thing.

Especially once Aemon caught sight of her.

"No," he growled, his flaming axe in hand. He had yet to put away his horns or crown, so the added axe was probably overkill. "She is mine. You can't have her. I don't care who you are to her, you'll tear her from my cold, dead hands."

"Aemon, no," I croaked as Lise worked red magic over me in a delicate spiral. "I—"

Those fire eyes met mine. "Remember how scared you were in France? How you screamed that she not step one toe near me? How is this any different?"

I wanted to kiss him and slap him in equal measure. "It's different because I ca-called her here."

Betrayal was stamped all over Aemon's face, and I had a feeling like mine had looked the exact same when Jay picked up that stupid stake.

"*Sang familial. Le sang de la soeur*," I murmured. "Lise needs family blood. She's my only family." The only one alive-ish anyway. "I didn't call her to die. I called her to live."

Aemon's fire eyes didn't waver, but his axe winked out of sight. "You missed part of that equation, Flower.

Lise didn't say sister. She said she needed blood of the 'made' family. Blood of the soulmate."

Sloane approached, slowly stepping around Aemon with her hands up.

"You don't need my blood, toots. You need his."

19

There was no such thing as soulmates.

If there was one thing I knew about this life, if there was one thing that was certain, it was that. There was no such thing as a person created just for you—written into the stars by Fate herself. They were a myth, a comforting lie.

"Bullshit."

Yes, that did come out of my mouth, and no, it was not on purpose.

"There is no such thing. You've got it wrong."

And what kind of spell required a true love soulmate? What was this, a fucking fairytale?

"You honestly believe we were not chosen for each other?" Aemon asked. "That we were not written into the stars themselves?" He crouched down to look me in the eye, his warm palm cupping my cheek. "Do you not see? Azrael put me in the one place only you would find me. In two thousand years no one ever disturbed me. Not once until you came."

He rubbed his thumb over my bottom lip. "Two thousand years and it was if you called me forth all on your own. Your heart, your mind. How could I not wake from my slumber? If that isn't a soulmate, I don't know what one is."

"I thought you said demons choose their mates."

His smile was soft. "We do. Our story may have been written before the dawn of man, but I chose you the moment I saw your mind. I choose you now."

I swallowed hard. "Does this mean... Is this... You said it wasn't time, Aemon. I don't—"

A cough cut off my words, the ripping ache of it threatening to tear me in two.

"Yes, well," he murmured, sitting on the shore and pulling me between his legs, curling his arm around my middle as my back pressed to his front, much like Mags had done with Tobin. "I think this curse may have made us jump the queue, Flower. You need my blood to heal, and when you take mine, I will take yours. Look at it this way, at least your sister was present at *your* wedding."

Wedding? My eyes flashed to Sloane, her smile the only thing keeping me tethered to the earth.

Afraid so, big sister. Fate told me to tell you to shit or get off the pot. I think that means she blesses the union or whatever, but that's just a best guess. She's a little hard to read, that one.

"We—"

"There isn't much time. The curse is moving too fast," Lise insisted through gritted teeth, the swirls of red magic staining her fingers scarlet.

"It is your decision, Flower. I know you don't think you have much of one, but you do."

And as hard as it was to admit it to myself, I did have a choice. Because unlike everyone else, death wasn't a hardship for me. I knew what I was getting on that front. I'd lose, sure, but it wasn't the same as the average person. Choosing Aemon—curse or not—wasn't exactly a hardship, either.

I might not have believed in soulmates, but I did believe that I was falling for him. I did believe that he would move heaven and earth for me. That he wanted me more than anything. That the thought of him not in this world would end me.

"I won't let you go, Flower," he said in my ear. "Not ever. And I won't leave you. I will listen to you and love you and be there for you. Always."

The truth was there as it had always been with Aemon. Nodding, I let myself believe it, too. "I choose you, Aemon. I don't believe in soulmates, but I do believe in you."

"*Très bien.*" Lise interrupted, a sweat breaking out on her forehead. "Slice your wrist. Feed her your blood. *Allons-y.*"

With an efficiency that was slightly frightening, Aemon sliced his wrist with his thumbnail and brought it to my lips. Coppery blood filled my mouth and I forced myself to swallow. As soon as it hit my throat, it was as if someone had taken jumper cables to my heart. My whole body jerked, but Aemon's grip got tighter as he held me still, forcing more of his blood down my throat.

"Again, Flower. You need more."

As if my body was at his command, I did as told, gulping down more and more of his blood. Breath filled my lungs as they repaired themselves, the cuts on my middle and arm and leg finally stitching back together, the muscle reforming all on its own. It was as if I was being drained of poison, the curse flowing out of me as his blood flowed in.

"More, my love," Aemon murmured, his lips at my neck. "Take more."

A moment later, his fangs were at my throat, piercing the flesh there in the most delicious way. I thought it would hurt, but instead, it felt so good I fought off the urge to moan around his wrist. If his blood healed me, his bite made me whole again. It filled me with hope, with joy, with the piece of my soul I'd thought had died.

It was a peace that had been missing since our time in the Underworld. A bliss. It was like coming home.

And then his lips were on mine, and I couldn't stop kissing him, our blood mingling together in a way that warmed me to my core. People thought what you needed was butterflies in your stomach, but they were wrong. Aemon thrilled me, sure, but more than that, I felt safe with him.

I never felt safe anywhere, but by Aemon's side? It was the safest I'd ever been.

"I now pronounce you husband and wife," Sloane joked. "You may kiss the bride."

But we were already kissing, and just because I could, I flipped her off as I kept right on making out with my man... demon... *whatever.*

The word "husband" would probably make the rotation into my vocabulary right around never, but we'd figure it out.

Probably.

"If the newlyweds are about done necking," Ingrid yelled from across the beach, "do you think we'd could break this blood curse sometime soon? If I hit Jay anymore, he's going to have brain damage."

That sobered me right up. I broke the kiss, only to

find Lise Dubois staring at me with a decent amount of pain in her eyes.

"What? Is something wrong? Did it not break right?" I asked, worry making a home in my gut.

She blinked, shaking her head. "No, it broke exactly as it was supposed to." Lise waved her hand in the air, pulling at it like there was an invisible thread she needed to yank. "With your friend, his curse is easy. Like a frayed sweater, all it takes is pulling a single piece of it and it falls apart."

She tipped her chin to Jay, who was coughing, vomiting up blackness before sitting up like he'd just woken up from the mother of all benders.

"Yours was tailored to you, made to latch onto your chaos and poison you from the inside out. Your friend was meant to give it to you. A final 'fuck you' from my daughter's son."

My chuckle was mirthless. "I want to be surprised, but he's becoming a bit predictable, is he not?"

Lise seemed less than thrilled with the whole situation. "I fear, child, that the closer he gets to the end, the less predictable he will become."

Aemon growled under his breath about hauling Bishop down to Tartarus and ripping him limb from limb, a sentiment I was totally onboard with. Because I hated to think just how right she was. And all I could do was look at Jay to be proven right. He'd tried so hard not to hurt anyone and still managed to damn near kill three people, myself included.

Ingrid helped him stand, but if a vampire could have a concussion, Jay sure as shit had one. Then the past few hours hit him like a freight train. Face already white as a sheet, he stumbled to his knees.

"Jimmy. I-I... Did I... Someone tell me I didn't kill him. Please."

Jay's eyes went to me first, then to Ingrid. Arms wide, head downcast, he offered himself to Ingrid like she was about to take his head.

"I should kick you in the balls," I growled, knowing damn well he could hear me. "Better yet, Ingrid, why don't you do it? He's so eager to hurt himself, why not make it good? Maybe if you hit him hard enough, he'll wake the fuck up."

Ingrid tapped her bottom lip like she was thinking about it, while Jay lowered his arms to protect his unmentionables. "Give him a minute. He may have brain damage after all."

Fair. "No, you did not kill Jimmy. Injure, yes, but not kill. You didn't kill Tobin either, but that one is a gray area since he got changed over to a vamp. If I let you see Jimmy, are you going to stop trying to off yourself, or do I actually need to get you a 5150?"

A 5150 was the code for an involuntary seventy-two-hour psychiatric hold for the suicidal. And damn if I ever thought I'd have to put him in one.

Jay's eyes left mine to turn to Ingrid. "You said that if I ever hurt someone, you'd take my head. That unless I gave myself over, you'd take Björn's, too. I thought... I was doing you a favor by not making you do it. I hurt him, Ing. Bad. And Tobin. How can you not want me out of your nest?"

"You were under a blood curse, dummy." Ingrid flicked him on the forehead—something I really wanted to do right then—before hauling him to his feet. "We've all been there. That wasn't you, and the fact that you went where you didn't hurt humans, where you tried to keep others safe? That's big, you doofus. And I'd be proud of you if I didn't want to knock you out again."

He seemed at a loss, and if I were being honest, so was I. There was only so much I could deal with, and now that he wasn't actively trying to kill himself, I was considering it a win.

Would I watch him like a hawk now? Yes.

Would I make Dahlia or somebody spell his ass so he could do no harm to himself?

Abso-fucking-lutely.

Jay returned his gaze to me, slowly crunching over the sand. "Do you think he'll... will he..." He swallowed hard, his throat working with what he wanted to ask. "Will he forgive me? Will either of them?"

"Jimmy begged me not to kill you. Me. Of all people. If there was anyone who is made to forgive, it's Jimmy Hanson. As far as Tobin, I don't know, but neither Acker nor Tobin ratted you out, so I'm thinking they know it wasn't really you in the driver's seat."

And because I couldn't stay mad at Jay to save my life, I pulled the idiot into a hug.

"I'll make you a deal. You promise to never make me watch you try and kill yourself for the rest of forever, and I'll think about forgiving you sometime in the next century. Sound good?"

He squeezed me back before pulling away.

"It's all kinda fuzzy. I don't remember much more than trying to make myself stop. Then you tackled me and I..." He rubbed his temple. "I scratched you. I tried so hard not to, but it was as if someone else was in control of my brain."

Oh, I had a guess who was in charge then, the slimy fucker.

"It's—"

I was going to say fine, but it wasn't. Nothing was fine.

Before I could continue that thought, Simon and Sloane hissed at the same time. Simon pulled back the sleeve of his flannel shirt, revealing a message burned into his skin.

His face went white as did Sloane's.

Oh, I didn't like this one bit.

Then the color returned to his face as his eyes went from green to black, the sclera gone as black fingers of his death magic trailed up his neck.

In all the time I'd known him, I'd never seen Simon Cartwright ready to commit murder. Now that I'd witnessed it, I had a feeling the news was just about as bad as it could get.

"The Night Watch is surrounded. They need us. Now."

Fuck.

20

The last time I was at the Night Watch's compound outside of Ascension, I'd been full of souls—thousands of them trying to break free of my very skin. I'd been dying, my body too fragile to hang onto them and no way to get them out.

A few months ago, I'd nearly died on this very property. Now? I was watching my friends struggle not to do the same.

Wolves—both in animal form and not—surrounded the compound, biting, scratching, fighting to get inside the walls. It was a four-alarm emergency, and this time, Lise didn't quibble when Simon latched onto her bicep and dragged her with us. No, she practically offered herself as tribute, aching to crush the likely new problem her grandson had caused.

Because Bishop *had* done this.

After being infected myself, after having that curse flow in my veins, I knew the scent of it. This was the same curse that had infected Jay and Jimmy. The same one that tore through the Dubois nest and the Monroe ghouls. It broke arcaners to their baser urges, it made killers out of good men.

And these shifters weren't just random people on the street or enemies from a past grievance. These wolves were the LeBlanc pack, used as cannon fodder to piss me off.

Well, mission fucking accomplished, you sadistic fuck. I'm real fucking mad now.

As much as Sloane wanted to help, she was bound by the job she now held. She could not interfere no matter how much she wanted to. But Simon and Lise? They were all over it.

Actually, it was a little frightening how quickly those two went from bitter enemies to war buddies in the blink of an eye. I'd once worried that I'd have to get in the middle of them about to kill each other. Now, I was sitting back in awe at them ready to tear the whole world apart.

It was also fucking scary how much Simon had prepared for just this moment. As soon as our feet touched down, Simon was hard at work pulling the dead from the ground like fucking daisies. And it wasn't like he'd yanked them from a cemetery or something. Oh, no. These bodies had been carefully and methodically planted here in the event he ever needed to have a horde of minions at his disposal.

The sky was already the full black of night, but as soon as Simon touched his feet to the ground, it seemed to breathe him in. The moon hid behind the clouds as the wind whipped through the field, and then the dead began to rise from the earth. Not from coffins or anything—no that would be too easy. No, they clawed from the earth, their rotten flesh and bones coming out of the ground like... like...

I'd love to say I was calm when Simon worked his magic. I would absolutely adore saying that I didn't lose my shit once, didn't want to claw my own skin off, or think my heart was going to fall out of my throat.

I'd love to, but I couldn't.

As soon as the bones started coming out of the ground, I was back in that tunnel with Bishop as he called a horde to come kill me. And even though not a single dead body even so much as sniffed in my direction, I stood there frozen, trying not to scream.

Aemon's arms wrapped around me, his deep voice saying words I couldn't process as I stared at my worst nightmare come to life.

Simon's power flowed through the entire grounds, and each zombie latched onto a wolf, yanking them back down, hanging onto ankles and legs, pulling them into the ground.

And beyond that army of shifters being held down by Simon's horde of zombies were five witches trying their damnedest not to die as they strengthened the ward around the house. Four of the witches were unknown to me, but one tiny blonde stood out like a sore thumb.

Fiona Jacobs.

There was no way a member of the Jacobs Coven should be anywhere near the Night Watch without a damn good reason. Unfortunately, I surmised that the reason was the mission I sent her feisty ass on in the first place.

Aces. If she got killed, her daddy would be up my ass until the end of time, and the absolute last thing I needed was Josiah Jacobs in my shit.

Jay, Ingrid, and Sarina held back behind me and Aemon, the fear of getting blood cursed again a very real thing. Sarina had yet to experience the full effects of Bishop's magic, but from personal experience, it was not a good time. Jay and Ingrid had a front-row seat for the destruction it caused and wanted no part of this fuckery.

Luckily, we had Lise on our side.

I regularly forgot just how old Lise Dubois was. If

Mags and Ingrid were older than Jesus himself, Lise had to have been three decades past ancient to have survived as long as she had. Blood mages weren't exactly on every street corner, either. Sloane's birth mother had been one, but I hadn't run across too many in my years in the arcane world.

And three seconds into Lise stepping up to bat, and I was damn glad that woman had never considered me an enemy. Her bullshit grandson was bad enough. I'd need actual god power, chaos, a fuck-ton of help, and a prayer to kick this woman's ass.

Blood-red magic rose from her hands as yelps and snarls rumbled from the field. The shifters were fighting against Simon's hold but there wasn't much of a fight to be had. Plus, I had a feeling Simon had no interest in killing innocent people just caught in the crossfire. No, his plan was to hold them still while Lise did her bit.

And that she did. A blanket of red power shot like an arrow from one shifter to another, each one falling to the ground and vomiting up blackness and blood just like Jay had, the putrid remnants of Bishop's spell nearly making me gag, too.

Wolves involuntarily shifted back to their human forms, the animals fading in a swath of gray smoke. Now in human form, some of them screamed at being held down by literal zombies, which I thought was fair.

"Hey, Simon," I croaked, trying to gather my courage just a little bit. "You might want to send your buddies back into the ground, maybe?"

Simon seemed to take in my likely pale face, sweaty brow, and galloping heart, and his eyes faded back to green. The death magic bled from his skin, crawling back down his neck. His pets released their hostages before crawling back down into the dirt where they came.

Note to self: Never come here again.

"This is what you fear?" Simon asked, his head tilted to the side like I was a puzzle he was working out. "My puppets? Slimy as they are, they can't hurt you. I only get this power from Death herself. Don't you know that? Every death mage does. They couldn't kill you. Not really."

As someone who had damn near died from a zombie horde, I begged to differ. "I think your information is a bit off." Because Bishop had damn near killed me. He'd damn near killed me *a lot.* "Or I need to punch my sister in the boob, because getting stabbed in the stomach with zombie bones was not fun for me. At all."

Neither was the swarming. Or the pulling at my clothes or... *Nope. Not going there.*

"Interesting."

I rolled my eyes. *Yeah, yeah, I was an anomaly.*

"No, you misunderstand. I take it Aemon helped you

survive?" At my nod, Simon's smile stretched across his face. "I think your sister was matchmaking."

Why, that little sneak. She was doing more than just getting Essex in that damn tunnel.

"Simon," Dahlia yelled from the front door, racing through witches and pack members alike to get to Simon. Three feet from him, she jumped, and he caught her, planting a kiss so hot on her lips I felt the heat from here.

Giving them some privacy, my gaze found a familiar face in the crowd. Fiona Jacobs was on the Night Watch's porch talking to Thomas Gao, the ancient vampire's expression as surly as ever. Picking through the crowd, I made a beeline for the Jacobs Coven princess.

Several questions hit my brain, but at the forefront was: What the fuck was she doing here? Fiona seemed to gather that, since as soon as she saw me, her face turned sheepish.

"I know what you're thinking," she said, her hands raised like she was going to ward me off.

My snort was indelicate, but I just couldn't muster the give a fuck. "Oh, I highly doubt that. I asked you to look for a witch. I don't see any mercenary witches here."

Thomas snorted, crossing his arms over his chest. "You're lucky we didn't kill you on sight. I'd love to hear exactly why you and yours showed up five minutes before all hell broke loose."

Pink hit her cheeks and she pulled at her collar a bit. "See, what had happened was that I went with a few of my father's guys to track Tobie Willis—the assassin that was hired to blow up the tunnel. She was a Knoxville Coven witch who had been up at the lake when all that mess went down. We cornered her outside of Dayton, and we were gonna bring her in, but when we tried, she kind of went batshit insane and started murdering people."

A big burly witch—Paul, I think it was—nodded, backing Fiona up. "It was crazy—and that's big coming from us. We've seen every kind of crazy a witch could go, but Tobie was off on one."

I didn't know Paul from Adam, but I had a feeling he'd seen some shit.

"We managed to break her wards," Fiona continued, "and I figured you wouldn't care if she was neutralized a bit, since she was, you know, killing people, but before we got in there, she... umm..." Fiona looked up at Paul who shrugged like he couldn't explain it, either. "Best I can describe it as, she went squish."

"Squish?"

Fiona gulped like she was trying to scrub the memory from her head. "Like a damn water balloon. There was blood and guts everywhere. It was as if she liquified and burst."

Thomas chuckled like he couldn't believe it, either. Centuries on the planet and he was still surprised.

"Fantastic." Pinching my brow, I tried not to be irritated a cracked-out witch got her comeuppance, but... I looked up at Aemon. "Blood curse? Again?"

He nodded. "Or she was the first."

That made more sense. Tobie had to have been spelled first before she attacked the LeBlanc pack.

"Well, we decided that watching the shifters she tried to kill was a good idea since ol' girl was a little bit in pieces, and I couldn't exactly bring her to you. The pack started rebuilding the tunnel, and then all of a sudden, damn near all of them shifted and headed here. I'm glad you guys showed up. I couldn't exactly ask Daddy to give them a call to let us in. If he knew I was talking to the Night Watch, he'd shit a kitten."

Lise appeared at my side, earning a deferential nod from Thomas. "Did you say that the witch burst?"

Fiona nodded, her eyes going a little wide at seeing the head of the arcane council just standing right in front of her.

But it was Lise's pain—pain that seemed to be stamped all over her—that made my stomach drop.

"I tried to figure it out, but this is the only thing that makes sense. I know who is helping him. I didn't want to believe it before but—" She swallowed hard, her hand pressing against her chest like she was trying to hold her heart in. "The magic is too similar. I-I can't help you anymore, Warden."

Lise turned before explaining, and tried to run, but Aemon caught her by the elbow. "Explain, madam, or we will be having a problem. Do you want a problem with me?"

She yanked at her arm, blood-red magic forming on her fingers, and then I got good and pissed.

A golden blade of light was at her throat before she could get off a single shot. "I get that you're having a personal crisis right now, and you've helped a bunch, so I'm real hesitant to cut your head clean off, but if you don't stand the fuck down and get a grip, I'm gonna throw that whole idea out the window. Just tell us what's going on."

Tears formed in Lise's red eyes before her magic died on the air. "My daughter. It's my daughter's magic. I cannot help you anymore. Please don't—" She squeezed her eyes closed, tears falling in rivers down her face. "Don't make me hurt her."

"How do you know?" I asked, my tone as gentle as I could make it. "Bishop is her son, it could—"

"I know my daughter's magic. No blood mage his age is that powerful. As weak as he is, he could not pull this off. Odette, though. She could. And she can hide—better than anyone. One of her favorite things to study was liminal spaces. You won't find her, and I can't... Not my daughter. Please."

"You'd rather save a murderer than help us? Daughter or not, she's helping him kill people, Lise." My delivery was less than kind, but the reality was there.

Lise sagged in Aemon's iron grip. "I would rather die on this spot than help someone kill my daughter."

Aces.

Aemon met my gaze before snapping his fingers, the mage's body going slack. He handed her over to Thomas. "You still have those high-tech cages in your basement, yes? It might be time for her to take a rest in one until we can figure out what to do."

But I already knew what to do, I just didn't quite know how to execute said plan.

Because if it was Bishop's mother helping him, I had a feeling I knew exactly where they'd made their home base. It made perfect sense to me. The witch was tasked with clearing out the tunnels, getting the LeBlanc pack out from what Bishop deemed his perfect hiding place. Hell, he and Essex had been in those tunnels together all those months ago when Bishop helped Essex escape the ABI.

Who was to say that hadn't always been Essex's hiding spot?

And why wouldn't he hide there? It was like the biggest "fuck you" there was, hiding in the one spot I was afraid of.

Thomas took Lise into his arms and swept inside, and I broke the news to Aemon.

"How much do you want to bet that in the tunnels under the LeBlanc pack house there is a nice little crossroads for them to hide out in?"

Fire lit in Aemon's eyes.

"All the gold in the world."

Perfect.

21

"You aren't going in there alone," Jay argued, yanking at my arm to get me to stop.

No, I was not going there alone, but I sure as hell wasn't going with him. I'd already watched his ass die in those tunnels once, and damn, if I was going to do it again.

"How about you stop telling me what I am and am not going to do and remember that I have seen enough of you in danger for the rest of forever, let alone for one damn day. You and Jimmy have gone through enough, okay? It's time for you to go check in on him and leave me to handle this shit."

Yes, I might have still been mad at the guy, but could anyone blame me? He'd damn near offed himself, and I was not going to watch as Bishop fucking La Roux finished the job for him.

Jay let go of my arm, stepping back. Granted, it was less about what I said and more because I had a giant demon at my back, who was staring at Jay's hand like he'd really enjoy lopping it off.

"Yes, and while you're enjoying your reunion with your partner, maybe contemplate just what I'll do to you if you happen to follow us like you're planning. I could put you to sleep now if you wish, or can I trust you to not be a flaming pain in my ass?"

Jay gritted his teeth, his eyes going red for a moment before bleeding back to the usual blue. "Damn mind readers. I—"

"Want to watch out for her, but you can't. Not where we're going. Undead things can't enter. Not without getting stuck on the other side."

I'd learned this with Oskar. It was why Bishop wasn't dead already. A fact we'd told him already. Twice. If only Jay would get it through his thick skull. The only other person we needed to make sure didn't follow us was Sarina.

"We need to go. Where's Sarina?"

"Umm..." Fiona broke in, her face as white as a sheet. That girl had all but disappeared while Lise was throwing her hissy fit and she was popping up now? Not good.

"Would Sarina happen to be the tiny ABI oracle lady? Because she may have made me give her one of my dad's umm... *transportation orbs*?"

I swear to Christ it was like talking to a teenager who had just gotten caught taking her daddy's Porsche, only if that Porsche was illegal as fuck. Those orbs had been banned in the twelfth century because they had an awful habit of making the user explode into a million pieces if the math was even slightly wrong. And if Sarina had grabbed it, she knew damn well who Fiona was and why she had the highly illegal artifact, too.

I'd wondered how they'd gotten here ahead of the pack. Now I knew.

Transportation orbs. Of all the...

Not my jurisdiction. Not my jurisdiction. Not my jurisdiction.

My eyes found Paul in this mess, his face just as guilty as hers. "Get her home. The last thing I need is her daddy thinking I talked y'all into being here." My glare returned to Fiona. "Which I did *not*. And when you actually get home, maybe think about what I said. You're better than this, Fiona. And you damn well know it."

But I couldn't give much time to either Jay or Fiona or whoever else might want something of me. We needed to get to Sarina before she did something stupid.

A moment later, Aemon's arm was around my waist,

and a second after that, we touched down in a place I would rather have never seen again.

But before I could gather the courage to go inside that godforsaken tunnel, a familiar presence appeared on my right. For the first time in months—no, *years*—I didn't jump.

"I know ya aren't goin' in there without me, lass." Hildy said, wincing as he prepared himself for me to flinch.

That little shit. He'd been doing it on purpose. *Later. I'd kick his ass later.*

"Yes, I am," I insisted. "You can't go in there without getting stuck. If that place is what I think it is, you shouldn't be within a mile of here."

Hildy drew up to his full height, which since he was older than dirt and people weren't quite as tall back then, put him right at my eye level. He sniffed, straightened his cravat, and slid his top hat onto his head. "I've been here before and made it out just fine. I swore I'd keep ya safe, lass. And that's exactly what I'm doing."

When Hildy got his mind made up about something, there was no changing it. I supposed it was a family trait.

"I don't care that you've married a Prince of Hell and he can watch out for ya. I've been doing this job the longest, and damn if I'm gonna fail ya now. I should have known about him, lass. I should have protected ya better, and now—"

But it wasn't Hildy's fault any more than it was mine. It wasn't my fault that Bishop had spelled me. It wasn't my fault that he manipulated every single thing about our relationship. It wasn't my fault that he plotted and connived and hurt me. It wasn't Hildy's fault, and it wasn't mine, either.

"He tricked us all. And if I'm not taking the blame for what he did to me, neither should you."

I was almost positive this feeling of clarity would fade when I was no longer looking my own personal nightmare dead in the face, so to speak. Positive that tomorrow—if it ever came—I'd start blaming myself for every time Bishop lied to me, stole from me, bargained away my mind and my peace for his gain.

But that was tomorrow's problem.

"What are the odds Sarina is alive and kicking and ready to lead us to victory?" I asked, staring at the mouth of the tunnel with a fair bit of trepidation.

Hildy followed my gaze as Aemon tightened his grip on my middle.

"I'd say about fifty-fifty. She took his lies hard, lass. She's been trying to see more, find out more about him. It's killing her that she was so blind to Bishop's lies."

Months ago, Sarina's visions had been damn near

blinded after she'd begged Jimmy for an amulet like mine. Mine worked perfectly, but Sarina's kept her visions away, which for someone who had relied on them for her whole life, was a huge problem.

Aemon grunted his agreement. "And she isn't seeing things like she used to. Even with the wards down and the necklace gone."

And who was to say that blame didn't fall at Bishop's feet, too?

We needed to get in there before she did something she either regretted or got her killed. Or both.

"You know he has that place booby-trapped up the vag," I grumbled, staring at the opening like it was going to kill me. Hell, it probably would. "I would like to make it in there and kill them without dying myself if possible."

And he was probably warded against ghosts, too, but I didn't say that. It was entirely possible that Bishop's hubris prevented him from thinking we'd figure his shit out, even with Sarina on our side. He'd been dicking with people so long, it was our only hope that he'd gotten sloppy.

"How about," my sister said, sneaking up on me in a way that Hildy had been unable to, "you think about it for just a second before you go in there?"

Sloane walked out of the shadows, scythe in hand,

wings out, her pale-violet eyes glittering in the night. *Oh, this was bad.* If she was here already, this was a no-good, very bad day.

But instead of a more ominous warning, she handed over her scythe with a gentle nod. "I would like you to borrow this for a little while."

Hand shaking, I closed my fingers around the wooden handle, the power of Death herself vibrating through my body. Yes, Azrael had given me some of his power, but Sloane had the lion's share. She had the wings, the powers, the... everything. I didn't begrudge her that, but the imbalance was there. She was doing a job I never wanted to do. She was important in a very different way than I was, and I wouldn't trade places with her for anything.

But... if this was what she felt every single day of her life? It would be tough *not* to be seduced by it.

"When the job is done, I'll be taking it back, but you need it more than I do right now." She slipped her arms around my shoulders, shoving Aemon out of the way for just a second. "When the time comes, don't be stupid like I was. Just kill him. No vengeance is worth him getting away. Remember that."

As ominous as that advice was, I still appreciated it. Sloane wasn't supposed to help, but she was. For me. I had no idea how to thank her.

"You can thank me by coming out of this alive, big sister. Now, you need a little cloaking, right?" She wiped away a tear from her eye as she gave me a knowing smile. "Hold hands, children."

I grabbed Hildy and Aemon's hands, and Sloane waved her fingers, a blanket of darkness settling over us like a cloak. I hadn't thought she would be so literal about it, but I wouldn't complain.

"That should get you in there, but once you cross into the liminal space, it will disappear. You'll be able to see the barrier, so don't cross it unless you're ready."

Swallowing, I followed her gaze to Hildy. She was warning him. Shit.

A sense of foreboding that hadn't really cemented itself in my gut yet reared its ugly head. But Sarina didn't have time to waste and neither did we.

"Stay safe in there," she murmured, her smile a touch worried.

I tightened my grip on the scythe. "We will."

But it was a lie. Safe was about as far away as it could get. And as the mouth of the cave swallowed us up, I had a feeling Sloane had changed about as much fate as she could. We'd have to do the rest on our own.

Months ago, when I was at this very antechamber, Hildy had scouted the way. Now that I knew what a crossroads felt like, I didn't have the need anymore.

Granted, that didn't stop him from doing it anyway, the familiar low light of him guiding my way, and Aemon's hand in mine the only things keeping me from running screaming from the joint.

The tunnel was still half-collapsed, the rubble making it slow going for a while as we climbed over boulders and through tight spots where the corridor had almost completely been cut off from the outside. And all the while I struggled to breathe, to think, praying that when it came time to finally fight him in this nightmare, I'd still have the oxygen in my lungs to do it.

We came to an open pocket of space before two more tunnels branched off. It was farther than I had ever been inside these caves, past where Jay had lost his humanity and where I had nearly taken my last breaths. Past where Bishop became a stranger and where Aemon had become something... more.

They can't hurt you. I only get this power from Death herself. Don't you know that? Every death mage does. They couldn't kill you. Not really.

I think your sister was matchmaking.

When had I realized that Aemon was on my side? When had I figured out that he gave a shit about me? Sloane had helped me trust a good man when I never thought I'd trust anyone ever again. Now he was my lover, my friend, my... *Nope, still not going there.*

Maybe I could get the courage to examine that when I wasn't dealing with my bullshit ex.

There were two paths in front of us. One way had the same energy I had felt in the catacombs, but the other had a power signature coming off of it that made all the little hairs on my arms stand on end. If I was a super-powerful blood mage helping my whacked-out son, where would I be hiding?

My grip tightened on Sloane's scythe, the urge to run through that damn tunnel swinging a real thing. Instead, I did the mature thing. The smart thing. In theory.

"Hildy, check that one, but be safe about it, yeah?"

Hildy's smile was devious, but he nodded all the same. "I can do that, lass."

A moment later, he zoomed through the tunnel, but when he came back, it was less info and more frantic hand waving to get in there. Hauling ass, we followed Hildy to a tucked-away chamber, hidden far from prying eyes and cloaked with enough magic, it had my chaos responding in fits.

The urge to burn everything had flames dripping from my very fingers.

Because behind that veil of magic was a circle, and in that circle were the desiccated husks of two mages, their deaths almost assured.

The information clicked in my brain in an instant.

Bishop had gotten so powerful so quickly.

The power and signature of the blood curses was so much like his mother's.

He had been abandoned to the ABI at birth.

Those weren't just random mages in that circle.

They were his parents.

22

"Odette Dubois and Armand La Roux," Hildy whispered. "I haven't seen these two in the same room in five hundred years."

That took me by surprise. "Jesus, fuck, Hildy. How old are you?"

My ghostly grandfather gave me a wicked smile. "I'll never tell."

I'd get it out of Sloane at some point. But first, we needed to break into this chamber and break the tie Bishop had on this circle. Because if we could cut him off from his power source, maybe it wouldn't be such a dick punch to lop his stupid head off.

Aemon had the same idea I had.

"If we had some blood of his line, we could break the circle," he mused, tapping his lip with his index finger.

"But I think the only way to get Lise's blood is to actually kill her, and I'm assuming you're opposed to that plan."

Kill a council head? Even I didn't want that kind of heat. "Option two?"

"Overload it," Hildy offered. "Put so much power into the barrier, that it shorts out."

While a good idea, it was also going to suck. Pouring that kind of power into the circle would give Bishop access to it until we could break it. It was dangerous—maybe too dangerous—but Bishop had to be stopped before he decided to take over the humans the next time.

"Is there an option three?"

Aemon threaded his fingers through mine before pressing a kiss to my temple, the fire on my skin not burning him in the slightest. I sort of loved that he was fireproof.

"No, Flower, there isn't."

Swallowing, I nodded. "It's going to take all three of us, isn't it? That's why Sloane didn't tell Hildy not to come. She knew it would take us all."

"Yes, lass," Hildy murmured, his grayed-out form turning Technicolor as the eyes of his skull cane began to glow. He placed a hand on my shoulder, far away from my burning hands. "It'll take us all, I think."

There was a real chance this wouldn't work. That we

would give too much of ourselves and... I could lose them both.

"I love you, Hildy. You kept me sane when I thought I was losing it. You protected me and guided me. I'll never forget it."

Hildy swallowed hard, his top hat bowing a little as he did so. "Right back at ya, lass. It has been the highlight of my life to see ya grow up. Wouldn't trade it for anything."

My throat clogged, I simply looked at Aemon, a helpless feeling bubbling in my chest.

"I know, Flower," he whispered, before dropping a gentle kiss to my lips. "You'll say it soon enough, and when you do, it won't be in a tunnel that still gives you nightmares and it won't be because you think we aren't going to make it. You will tell me you love me when you're ready and not a moment before. It's one of the many things I love about you, Darby Jean Adler. Trust me, Flower. I'm a patient man. I can wait."

Then my throat became unstuck, the truth flying out of my mouth before I could stop it.

"I love you, too," I breathed, wanting him to know as soon as I finally let myself believe it. And I didn't want to die without saying it—whether it was in five minutes or a thousand years.

A sweet sort of pride hit his expression as if he never expected me to say those words to him ever.

"Then let's do this so you can tell me with the moon shining on us instead, yes?"

Blinking, I nodded, focusing all my energy on the barrier that kept the circle away from prying eyes, the chaos mingling with Hildy's wealth of power and weaving through with Aemon's darkness. All three mixed together, they cut through that feeble barrier like tissue paper.

But that wasn't the problem.

The barrier was child's play compared to the juiced-up circle that drained Bishop's parents. There would be no breaking it, but Hildy had been right. We did need to overload it. I knew it better than anyone: no one could hold too much power under their skin without it eating them alive.

I took as much power as I could from Aemon and Hildy, giving it to the circle, pouring as much as I could give of myself. The fatigue hit first, buckling my knees as I tried not to stop. Blood dripped from my nose, my breaths coming in shallow pants, my bones nearly breaking under the strain. Hildy and Aemon followed me down, hitting the dirt right next to me.

Hildy had lost all his color, his cheeks sunken and his

eyes damn near dead. He began to wane, even the gray visage fading from my sight.

And Aemon...

The fire was dying in his eyes, his skin as gray as Hildy's, blood running from his nose. In that moment I felt as selfish as I could possibly have been. I was hurting him to do this, and that about broke my heart. The three of us didn't have enough juice to break the circle. And if we stopped now, it could kill us all, and if it didn't...

We'd never get that power back. But if we succeeded, there was a chance we'd win. We'd get everything we'd given. In theory.

There was only one thing left to draw from.

Tightening my fingers around Sloane's scythe, I ripped the power from the wood itself, shoving it into the circle like the blade it was. The entire tunnel trembled with it, the circle shredding as we were all knocked back by our own powers.

Breath flooded my lungs as the chaos I'd given away filled my very bones, healing me, charging me.

"Aemon, Hildy, tell me you're okay," I croaked, rolling over as the aches and pains drained from me.

A decidedly unsolid Hildy peeled himself from the ground, top hat and cane gone, but he was still with us. "Here, lass."

Aemon's hand appeared in front of my face, hauling

me up from the dirt so he could inspect me. "You're all right. Gods, Flower. I thought we'd... we'd..."

Enveloping me into the tightest hug, he dropped kisses to whatever skin he could reach. "Never again. I never want to watch you go through that again."

And I never wanted to see him give so much for me and me be the one to just take. "Same."

Before we could get too comfortable, a rage-filled scream rocked the tunnel. I would have thought it was Bishop if it weren't for the decidedly feminine quality to it.

Sarina.

I fought off the urge to run. We needed to be smart about this. We couldn't just waltz in there and get killed —it didn't matter if Bishop wasn't as strong anymore.

"Stay here, Hildy. You remember what Sloane said. If you cross, you won't make it back out."

Hildy's eye twitched. "My ears work just fine, lass. I heard her."

That wasn't the same as a promise, but it would have to do.

Aemon and I traversed the tunnel, mincing through cracks and fallen rocks to the one place that made my skin crawl. An eerie light bloomed from the crossroads, as the sounds of fighting echoed through the cavern. My feet had a mind of their own as they moved us faster. I ignored everything: the sights, the ghosts, the *things* that seemed to lurk in the corners of my vision, heading toward the sound of Sarina's screams.

Rounding the corner, it was all my nightmares wrapped up in a little bow. Sarina was fighting for her life against a monstrous-looking Bishop, the death magics had done a number on him here. The blackness stained his once-handsome face with the traces of the grave, his mouth and eye sockets as dark as pitch.

His fingers, blackened with the rot of his magic, clawed at Sarina, blood welling from the cuts on her face as she struggled against his hold. Anything that had once been appealing in him was long gone. His hair was greasy, his skin—what wasn't degenerated from his power overload—was sallow as if his liver was failing.

"What did you do to me, you little bitch?" he growled in her face, murky spittle hitting her cheek as she fought him.

She needed to get away from him, and Bishop... he needed to just fucking die.

"Not a damn thing," I called, alerting him to my presence. "Me, however, well, I flipped your breaker, so to speak. How ya feeling without your little battery juicing you up, asshole?"

Faster than I thought he could move, he had Sarina up and against his body, using her as a shield.

Yep, the only way on this green earth I could have fallen for that man is if he spelled me to do it.

"You're supposed to be dying," he sputtered, his hate palpable in this confined space. "Yo-you needed me to break your curse. You—"

Aemon's laugh echoed off the stone walls while I stared at him aghast. "You poisoned me with a curse that could only be cured by the blood of my soulmate. Di-did you make that curse, tailor it to me, and then think it was *you* I needed?"

Aemon held his middle he was laughing so hard, tears coming out of his eyes. Me? I was horrified. Aemon? He was just cutting it up like Bishop was a fucking comedian.

"You think after all your spells and all your coercion, you were her soulmate? That you could cheat her heart into loving you? You could cheat Fate? Have you learned nothing, mate? People without a soul can't love, and they for damn sure can't have a soulmate."

"Fuck you. What would you know about it, demon?" Bishop snarled, a blackened blade forming in his hand as he put it to Sarina's throat.

"Enough to know Darby is my wife. You didn't break her curse, mage," Aemon growled, his flaming axe forming in his hand as his horns and crown formed on his head, his body enlarging into the dark smoke monster that had saved me so many times. "I did."

Bishop roared his displeasure, but he didn't attack. No, he backed up, jostling the blade against Sarina's throat.

"The Night Watch lives, the pack is safe, Jay and Jimmy are alive, so is just about everyone else. And you're out of power," I taunted. "Tell me—what else do you have, Bishop?

"You think you're so smart," he replied, shaking his head. "You spent months chasing your tail. Months. I got Essex free. I got Davenport out of the way. I got the LeBlanc pack to attack the witches. It was me who convinced Mariana to open the veil. And every step of the way, you've been chasing clues and in the dark, all the while *I've* been pulling your strings."

Fitting Sloane's scythe in my hand, I took a step to the left. "Except Essex is dead and Mariana is, too. So is your buddy Nero and everyone else who thought it would be a good idea to test me. For all your plans, you aren't that smart."

"And ya aren't that observant, either," Hildy said from his left, startling him enough that my grandfather could rip Sarina out of his arms and toss her in my direction.

Bishop slashed at Hildy, but he'd already gone non-corporeal, the mage's blade slicing through air. Aemon and I advanced at once, his axe at the ready while I ached to bury Sloane's scythe into his gut.

But even though Hildy caught him by surprise, Bishop didn't stay that way for long. Rounding on us, he parried our blows with a blade of his own, spinning, slashing, he tried to fight us off. That's when chaos decided to join the party.

Flames fell from Sloane's scythe as I circled Bishop, waiting for the perfect moment to strike. Those flames grew along the tunnel, reaching for his feet like little fingers. I was getting him one way or another.

"That chaos should've been mine. Your power should have been mine," he snarled, slashing at Aemon while railing like a loon. "You were *mine*."

He kicked at a flame that had reached his shoe, the burn taking his focus just long enough for Aemon to put his flaming axe into Bishop's gut. Eyes wide and wheezing, his magic faded from his hand, his blade disintegrating into a pile of oily magic.

Aemon spun, holding Bishop still just for me. It was like a present almost. Black blood fell from Bishop's mouth as he struggled for air, his fear-filled and feeble body trying his damnedest to get away from Aemon, to try and escape. But there wasn't a bit of a soul left in that body. It had been bargained and burned away from years of double-crosses and double-dealings.

"I was never yours, Bishop," I said softly, considering just what I'd do to him now that I had him all to myself. There were so many things I could do. So much pain I could inflict.

When the time comes, don't be stupid like I was. Just kill him.

Sloane's words rattled through my brain.

Okay, little sister. You win. I'll play it smart just this once.

"And you'll never hurt anyone else ever again."

Bishop laughed—the fucker actually laughed. "You're not going to kill me, Adler. You're too we—"

And instead of making him suffer, instead of glutting myself on his pain, and instead of letting him finish that fucking sentence, I hefted Sloane's scythe and cut his head clean off his shoulders.

His skull spun as it hit the ground, desiccating far faster than I thought it would.

It was over.

He was finally dead.

So why did the relief not come?

It didn't come because I knew exactly what I would have to sacrifice to walk out of here. Meeting Hildy's gaze, I fought off the urge to punch him in the face.

We warned him, but still, he came here. Why?

I hadn't realized I'd asked that aloud until Hildy answered me.

"Because I swore to Killian that I'd look after you. I swore I would protect you, and damn if I was going to let that bastard take someone else from you. Not again, lass."

The tunnel rumbled, signaling that maybe we should get out of here, but...

"Time to go, Flower," Aemon murmured, guiding me to the barrier before passing an unconscious Sarina and picking her up, too.

"No, no, put me down." Hildy. He couldn't come with us. He—

"I'm already dead, lass. I knew what I was signin' up for coming in here. Plus, you don't need me anymore. You've got your family and your friends. You don't need some ghost lurkin' around all the time I—"

Aemon rounded a corner, stopping short when Sloane appeared in front of him. Without hesitation, he passed over Sarina who lay limp in Sloane's arms. Stepping over the barrier, he took Sarina back, pressing a finger to her chest like he'd once done to me.

Instantly, the wounds at her neck closed and she coughed up black goo, her gasping breaths a far sight better than unconscious silence.

"My scythe?" Sloane asked, her hand held out. Reluctantly, I passed it over, but I didn't want to. I wanted to hold it hostage until she brought Hildy back, until she...

Raising an eyebrow, she reached across the barrier, latching onto Hildy's arm before hauling him out of the crossroads with a smile on her face.

"Consider this me flipping off Fate for you."

In the end, we needed to move fast.

Saving Bishop's parents had been at the bottom of my list, but Aemon brought up a good point. "It can't hurt to check, Flower. Imagine what it will do to your conscience if you let this place collapse on them."

Grumbling because I knew he was right, we hauled ass to see if they had even made it after Bishop's draining. Armand was a pile of ash, but Odette was still breathing. Maybe if we brought her back, it would take the sting out of Lise having a pariah as a grandson.

Taking her with us, we skipped the trek and used Aemon to get gone. A moment later, I was breathing fresh Tennessee mountain air as the entire tunnel system decided to collapse. But just to be on the safe side, I figured sealing that place up nice and tight for the rest of forever sounded good.

Letting the chaos take the wheel, I imagined every lock turning, every bolt hitting home, every key being thrown in the deepest, darkest dungeon there was. If there was anything alive in there, it wasn't coming out and nothing else was getting in.

Ever.

As soon as that tunnel was gone, the relief I'd been missing finally decided to show up. The knot in my gut loosened, and the burn that seemed to always be there began to fade. It was as if I had been granted my life again.

Aemon's arm surrounded my shoulders. "You know what this means, right?"

Please say vacation. Please say vacation. Please say vacation.

"I get to take you to a beach somewhere with lots of food and very little clothing."

My fingers fisted in his shirt, ready to tear it off his body at the first glimpse of privacy. "That's what I was hoping you'd say."

It turned out that there was a whole lot of shit we had to do before we could even think of going away.

Naturally, Sloane and Hildy decided to fuck off while Aemon and I did the dirty work.

First, we needed to bring Odette to Lise. Considering the ancient blood mage was trying to dismantle the Night Watch's dungeon with her bare hands, it was pretty easy to distract her with the shiny that was her daughter. All we had to do was hand her over, and the woman was instantly appeased, calming as if she had been given a gift.

While Odette was still in bad shape, I figured the bad blood between the head of the council and I was now a thing of the past.

"When she wakes up, tell her that Bishop and Armand La Roux have both passed. If she feels some kind of way about that, please remind her that her son drained his father to death and was trying to do the same to her."

Lise's surprise was what caught me off guard. "She— she didn't do this? But the magic, the signature—"

"Was Bishop using her power to piss me off. She's lucky to be alive."

Lise cradled her daughter in her arms, pushing back her dark hair to kiss her forehead. "Thank you. I owe you."

Pivoting on a heel, I made my way out of the Night

Watch's dungeon. "You're damn right you do. And I'll collect. Later."

The next order of business was checking on Sarina in the med bay. A very crowded med bay to say the least. Harper was fussing all over her, dabbing at the healed cut on her neck and scolding the oracle about using untested artifacts.

"You could have died," Harper hissed, wiping at the blood until Sarina's neck was damn near raw.

"I didn't," she cooed, stilling Harper's hand.

The empath's eyes narrowed. "You—"

Sarina yanked at the smaller woman's shirt, pressing a searing kiss to Harper's mouth to shut her up. The lip-lock lasted a solid thirty seconds before the oracle broke the kiss to a very dazed and blissed-out Harper. "I *didn't*. Now will you quit yelling at me? I believe it's Darby's turn."

Pursing my lips, I shrugged my shoulders. "Do I need to tell you how dumb and irresponsible and downright dangerous what you did was?"

Because I had a feeling she knew all too well.

"No. Bishop nearly lopping off my head taught that lesson far better than you could."

I crossed my arms. "Did you learn it?"

Sarina waggled her hand at me. "I'd say about fifty-

fifty. Was it stupid and reckless? Yes. Did it get you to get off your ass and come save me? Also, yes. I'd say it worked out in the end."

Her smile told me she had far more inside information than she was willing to let on.

Fair enough.

"You know where Dave is in all this mess?"

I'd need to tell him his tunnel system was locked up tight and he wouldn't get it open. Ever. In fact, moving would be a good idea.

Her gaze got that far-off quality to it. "He's upstairs chatting up Emrys. Oh... nope. He's umm... busy. Maybe talk to him later?"

Did she mean that Dave and Emrys were... *Okay then.* "I'll call him later maybe. Yeah. Later."

It took an hour, but we managed to make it out of the Night Watch. But that was only after Ingrid yelled at me for killing Bishop without her, not saying anything when I left, and all that other bullshit.

Taking my life into my hands, I shut her up by giving the little gremlin a hug.

"I love you, too. Now can I go on vacation, or do you want to yell at me some more? Bishop is dead, I need a break and I hav—"

"A hot demon husband to bone on your honeymoon?"

No part of that sentence should have come out of the mouth of someone who looked eight years old, and I would need brain bleach just to unhear it.

"Yes," Aemon growled, his patience also wearing thin. "And you're delaying it."

Ingrid gave him an unrepentant grin. "You won't kill me, Prince. Your wife loves me too much."

And with that, the little shit skipped away, probably to start some chaos somewhere.

Tracking down Jay and Jimmy was less eventful. The pair of them were in the middle of Jay's living room, cuddled on a magically repaired couch and watching TV. Jay was sipping on a blood bag while Jimmy was half-listening to the show and drawing on a tablet.

They both looked up when we appeared, leaping off the couch like the damn thing was on fire as soon as Aemon's darkness faded. Jay ripped me out of Aemon's arms and hugged me so tight I creaked. The pressure intensified when Jimmy added to the mix.

"Holy shit," Jay mumbled. "You made it. I swear I thought Ingrid was going to shit a kitten when she found you gone. She told me to go home and relax but she'd keep watch and—"

"I'm okay. He's dead. It's over."

Jay pushed me back, staring at me like I was a

wizard or something. "For real? You really did it? And he isn't going to come back or crawl out of Hell or anything?"

I highly doubted it.

"I cut off his head with Death's scythe. I'd say it's pretty permanent."

It was over. I was done.

And it would hit me sometime that life was going to get easier. Maybe when I could breathe again, it would be true—I'd believe it. But for now, I had a family, I had friends, and I had Aemon.

When I was rested, I'd come back to Knoxville. I'd police this town, and I'd make sure there was never another Bishop La Roux. I'd make sure the streets were safe.

But first, I was going on vacation for a good long while, and the boys would hold down the fort.

"Come on, Flower," Aemon urged, pulling me out from under Jay and Jimmy and into his arms. "It's high time you took me on that holiday you promised me."

Narrowing my eyes, I crossed my arms over my chest. "I don't remember promising a vacation for you. I said *I* was going on vacation. No one said anything about you coming."

Growling, Aemon swept me off my feet, and I let out a peal of laughter. Pressing a kiss to his beautiful mouth,

I decided to let him off the hook. Or maybe... put him on one.

"Fine," I sighed. "Make it a honeymoon then."

Aemon's eyes lit up as a devilish smile pulled at his lips. Damn, I loved that smile.

"As you wish, Flower. As you wish."

THE END

This concludes the Grave Talker Series.
Thank you so much for reading. I can't express just how much I have adored writing Darby Adler and her ragtag bunch of friends.

However, if you would love to see a special glimpse of Darby & Aemon on their very much-needed vacation, turn the page for an epic **Grave Talker Bonus Scene**. *I hope you enjoy it!*

If you loved Darby & Aemon and would like to see more from the Jacobs Coven, stay tuned for **Curses & Chaos** *and all the crazy, witchy shenanigans that is to come. I hope you're buckled in to see Fiona contend with the* *aftermath of an accidental Hell gate snafu, life as a witchy mob princess, and her sinfully hot, totally clueless shifter mate.*

Want the skinny on future releases without having to follow me absolutely everywhere on social media?

Text "LEGION" to (844) 311-5791

BONUS SCENE

Dear Reader,

I hope you enjoyed the Grave Talker Series. Darby Adler has a very special place in my heart, and I am absolutely ecstatic for you to read more about her and her favorite demon prince.

I have an extra special bonus scene for you as a thank you for reading. All you have to do is click the link below, sign up for my newsletter, and you'll get an email giving you access!

SIGN UP HERE:
https://geni.us/db-bonus

Love Fiona? You'll see her again in
CURSES & CHAOS
The Lost Witch Book One

If the ABI finds me, I'm dead.

Agent or not, when your dad is the head of the most notorious arcane crime family in the country, no one believes you when you say you didn't open that gate to Hell on purpose.

Now, I'm practically glued under enough null wards to

hide a god and stuck with a stupidly sexy shifter of a jailer who hates my guts.

When my former employer comes sniffing around, not only does my captor keep me alive, but we find out that our pasts are far more connected than either of us realize.

And the lies we've been told could kill us both.

Preorder Now!

Coming May 23, 2023

Dying to learn more about Darby's sister, Sloane?
Check out...

NIGHT WATCH

Soul Reader Book One

I'm a killer. He's a bounty hunter. A match made in Hell. Literally.

Waking up at the foot of your own grave is no picnic... *especially when you can't remember how you got there.*

A year ago, I was a college senior still living with my

parents. Now? I'm the boogeyman of Ascension, TN, snapping up rogues and draining them dry.

That is until I'm ensnared by a mysterious bounty hunter whose blood and body I crave.

We'll likely kill each other once it's all said and done, but until then, he's bound to keep me on the straight and narrow.

Unless I can convince him to follow me to the dark side.

What? We have cookies over here.

Grab Night Watch today!

THE ROGUE ETHEREAL SERIES

an adult urban fantasy series by Annie Anderson

Enjoy the the Grave Talker Series?
Then you'll love Max!

She's brash. She's inked. She has a bad habit of dying... *a lot.* She's also a Rogue with a demon on her tail and not much backup. This witch has a serious bone to pick.

Check out the Rogue Ethereal Series today!

THE PHOENIX RISING SERIES

an adult paranormal romance series by Annie Anderson

Heaven, Hell, and everything in between. Fall into the realm of Phoenixes and Wraiths who guard the gates of the beyond. That is, if they can survive that long...

Living forever isn't all it's cracked up to be.

Check out the Phoenix Rising Series today!

JOIN THE LEGION

EXCLUSIVE SNEAK PEEKS,
GIVEAWAYS, BOOK DISCUSSION.
COME FOR THE BOOKS.
STAY FOR THE MEMES.

To stay up to date on all things Annie Anderson, get exclusive access to ARCs and giveaways, and be a member of a fun, positive, drama-free space, join The Legion!

facebook.com/groups/ThePhoenixLegion

ACKNOWLEDGMENTS

A huge, honking thank you to Shawn, Barb, Jade, Angela, Heather, Kelly, and Erin. Thanks for the late-night calls, the endurance of my whining, the incessant plotting sessions, the wine runs... (*looking at you, Shawn.*)

Basically, thanks for putting up with my bullshit.

Every single one of you rock and I couldn't have done it without you.

ABOUT THE AUTHOR

 Annie Anderson is the author of the international bestselling Rogue Ethereal series. A United States Air Force veteran, Annie pens fast-paced Urban Fantasy novels filled with strong, snarky heroines and a boatload of magic. When she takes a break from writing, she can be found binge-watching The Magicians, flirting with her husband, wrangling children, or bribing her cantankerous dogs to go on a walk.

To find out more about Annie and her books, visit www.annieande.com

facebook.com/AuthorAnnieAnderson

twitter.com/AnnieAnde

instagram.com/AnnieAnde

amazon.com/author/annieande

bookbub.com/authors/annie-anderson

goodreads.com/AnnieAnde

pinterest.com/annieande

tiktok.com/@authorannieanderson

patreon.com/annieanderson

Printed in Great Britain
by Amazon

40758217R00169